Early June

Mike Williams

It was a cool day for a ball game. The temperatures usually reached the low seventies at this time of year, but on this day the temperatures were in the low sixties. Up until now, Unionville had dominated us. The ball game had bounced back and forth all day. The bases were loaded for Franklin High School and down six to five. Julio stepped up to the plate to hit.

As for me, I was over in the on deck circle because I was the next batter up. For those who don't know, the on deck circle is a small circle where the next batter up stands and waits to hit. I stood in admiration as Julio stepped up to bat. He was a big kid who stood at a height of 6'4" and weighed around 220 pounds with strong well defined arms. He was an intimidating foe for any high school pitcher.

I'm sure some of you may be asking how I fall into this story. Well, my name is Mike Williams. For the last two years, I started at third base for the Franklin Wildcats. When I look back on my two years as a teammate with Julio, I can't help but think about how good we were as a team. At the same time, it saddens me to think of how the students at Franklin High treated Julio and his brother. I can even admit many of us were not the best teammates, especially at first.

Franklin was a small farming community south of the university town of Carbondale. Before Interstate 57 was built in the 1960s, the town of Franklin was a notorious Sundown town. What's a Sundown town? I'll never forget the reaction of my elementary teacher when I asked them what a Sundown town was after I heard my grandpa utter the phrase. Talk about an uncomfortable teacher. Looking back, they never really answered my question. Apparently, prior to the establishment of Interstate 57, the police would often stop minorities as they passed through Franklin. If they were lucky they wouldn't be stopped, which was rare. If they were stopped after Sundown, their chances of making it out of town that night decreased. Some were unlucky not to even make it out of town at all. Yep, I remember listening to my grandpa share stories of lynchings which blew my mind. Lynchings!

In retrospect, I never thought twice about someone zipping around town with a Confederate flag blowing in the breeze, another student or adult using some derogatory term about African Americans or other minorities, or in

4

simple conversations ministers or others in town suggest their desire for minorities to learn their place in society. Yep, that was the norm in Franklin for the longest time.

Between the 1960s and Julio and his family's arrival, very few minorities lived in the town. Hell, if I was an African American and I knew the history of Franklin, I surely wouldn't have moved to the town. It became the norm and the expectation that minorities lived in one of the neighboring towns like Clariton. Those that did attempt to move in were made to feel quite unwelcomed. Well, in the years since playing with Julio, I saw Franklin wasn't the norm and neither was Julio. They both were the exception. Sadly, it took Julio, Jeremy, Alexa, and certain events that happened during my last two years of school to slowly open my eyes to the world. I am just thankful I was able to share in Julio's journey, even though it was much bumpier than it should have been.

As Julio made his way to home plate, he looked to his left. He probably hoped to make eye contact with his girlfriend, Alexa. Curious, I looked towards the bleachers myself. It made me smile when I noticed her scream at the top of her lungs in support of Julio.

Julio walked behind the umpire and whispered, "Great

day for a ball game."

The umpire looked at Julio through his mask. "Yeah, it is."

Coach Wilson called Julio's name from third base. Julio turned and glanced towards his coach. He noticed Coach Wilson slowly walk down the baseline. Eventually the two met halfway between home plate and third base.

Coach Wilson looked him straight in the eye and smiled.

"Julio, this is your chance. Show everyone here what you're about. Relax and have fun up there."

Coach Wilson turned and made his way back to his spot by third base. Julio walked slowly towards the batter's box to hit.

2

School had just finished for the year. Julio was enthusiastic about the summer. Both he and his brother hoped to play ball over the summer. As a sophomore, Julio had earned a varsity letter from the school of West Aurora. As mentioned before, Julio was 6'4" and didn't have an ounce of fat on him. Thank goodness he was a nice guy. Otherwise, he could have been easily the school bully. He was quiet as well. Though a kid of few words, when he spoke, he meant business. Maybe that's one reason why I and others grew fond of him over time. He had an easy going personality as well. He was never quick to temper, unless his brother pushed his buttons of course. The girls seemed to like him as well. I mean, he was a good looking guy. What really set him apart from others was his work ethic though. Damn, the guy was a hard worker.

As mentioned, his sophomore season had just ended at West Aurora. The school was known for its strong baseball tradition. Like Franklin High School, West Aurora always had a good baseball team. It was actually newsworthy when the team wasn't good. Unlike Franklin, which had a small school population, West Aurora produced more college and professional baseball players. Actually, Franklin had never produced any professional players until Julio and his brother moved to town. Sadly, Julio and West Aurora ended the year with a loss to their regional rival, Oswego, another elite northern Illinois team, but things looked bright.

As he and his brother, Jeremy, walked home from school for the last time, they talked about summer and their travel ball plans. Both of them loved the game and would do anything to play it. Their parents and coach knew it.

As they approached the house, they joked about what their mom might be cooking. They never really appreciated their mom's cooking until they were on their own. To be honest, I was very much the same. Once I had to cook on my own, I could not wait to go home and visit my mom and dad.

"Hey Julio, do you think we'll have chicken tonight?" Jeremy mumbled.

"I don't know," Julio replied as he patted his brother on his back. "Let's get some catch in, I haven't thrown in a couple of days."

As much as Jeremy liked to play catch with his brother, he dreaded it because Julio threw the ball hard. Often times, the two threw for hours on end.

Jeremy was two years younger than his brother. He stood at 5'10", considerably smaller than his brother in size and weight, but bigger than many of his classmates.

Inside, Julio heard his mom on the phone. I guess his dad worked at the local bank. Apparently he made pretty decent money. Enough that Julio's mom could stay at home. This compared to my dad who probably made half as much. That didn't keep my mom from hardly working though.

"Are you sure this is the only option?"

There wasn't a reply... or at least not one Julio could hear.

"How do you think the boys will feel about it?"

There was a pause.

"Well, if you think it's for the best that's what we'll do. Just come on home and we can talk to the boys about it." She hung up the phone and noticed Julio standing in the hallway. His eyes were as wide as saucers.

"Who was that?" Julio asked, pointing at the phone.

"Your father."

3

Early June

Mike Williams

Their dad finally came home. Not long after arriving home, he called them into the living room. To their surprise, their dad had them sit down on the couch across from him and their mom.

"Boys, I have some news," he said somberly.

Quiet filled the air.

"We're moving."

For a moment, the boys were speechless.

Move? Where! What about baseball! This cannot be happening, Julio thought to himself.

Julio looked at his dad firmly.

"Where? Somewhere close I hope!"

"Son, trust me, I'm not happy about this."

Julio interrupted him.

"Where are we moving?" He asked with a quivering voice.

Mr. James tightened the grip on his wife's hand for reassurance. "We're moving to southern Illinois. The town is called Franklin."

"Julio and Jeremy were distraught. They didn't know what to think. A silence that seemed to last for an eternity filled the room. Then, as if some invisible tape that was holding the brothers together was cut, the anger rushed out."

"Where in the world is Franklin?!" Jeremy chimed.

Julio looked at his brother. "No. No way. This can't be happening. I have two more years left here in Aurora! I made the varsity! Jeremy will be playing ball next year! This sucks!"

"Son, I know you're not happy, but we really didn't have a choice in the matter."

There was a momentary pause.

"Boys, trust me, we'd stay here for four more years if we could, even twenty, but we can't. The bank has relocated your dad to another branch and he doesn't have much say in the matter."

Julio began to open his mouth as if he was going to speak, but his mom continued. "Julio, you need to step up. Don't think baseball is the only thing out there. Besides, this may be a great chance for you."

Tears began to run down Jeremy's cheeks. Julio looked at him, then his parents. Julio put his arm around his brother.

"Well, where in the world is this town of Franklin located anyways?"

Mr. James took out his phone and typed in the town of Franklin. He zoomed his map on the phone out to show all of Illinois.

"There it is."

Julio sighed.

There it is.

He pointed to a small dot off of Interstate 57 below the city of Marion. The boys glanced at the map for a moment.

Julio glanced up.

"How big is Franklin?"

His dad paused so everyone could see the location before he answered Julio's question. "Not very big, maybe five thousand."

Julio looked at his brother, then his mom, followed by his dad. "Are you serious?"

Mr. James paused. "Yes, the town is small, but it will be okay. We'll adjust."

He paused.

"Look, I know you guys don't want to move, but as your mom stated, we don't have much of a choice. We will be packing up in a few weeks."

Julio's jaw dropped.

"A few weeks? What am I going to do about summer baseball?"

4

Mid July

Mike Williams

Julio could tell it was going to be a warm day. As he slowly rolled out of bed, he took a deep breath as he glanced towards the horizon. After admiring the sunrise, he looked at his brother.

"Hey Jer, I'm going to go for a run. You wanna join?"

Even though the house had plenty of room, the two shared a room. It was always that way. The two brothers were close, so it was never an issue.

"Nah, not today," Jer grunted as he covered his face with his pillow. I would have taken the lazy way out as well. I never liked to run.

Julio shrugged his shoulders, threw on his shorts and t-shirt which read *West Aurora* across the front, and his red shoes. He jumped to his feet and made his way to the bedroom door. He stopped and looked at his brother who was still in bed. Julio picked up a pillow and threw it at his brother and grinned as he walked out the door.

He refused to believe the family was about to move. Sadly, he could not deny the boxes which were found throughout the house. The realization painfully began to sink in. Thankfully, the family was not set to move until after the July Fourth holiday, which allowed Julio and his brother to play summer ball with their friends.

As he approached the base of the stairs, he noticed his mom and dad in the kitchen. Each of them were holding a cup of coffee. Mr. James looked at his oldest son.

"Is everything alright, son?"

Julio glanced at them, then at the rest of the house.

"Yeah, I'm fine. I'm just going for a run before it gets too warm. Talk to you in a few." And with that, he was out the door.

He bound down the steps and up the main street. Normally he didn't run by the school for whatever reason, but this was not a normal day. He passed Hancock Street and Butterfield Lane. In no time, he reached the school parking lot.

The population of the school was rather large, especially compared to dinky Franklin High School. West Aurora's school population was nearly 1,500 students. He had always wanted to play for the West Aurora Wildcats. Ironic that the two schools had the same mascot.

Finally, he reached the field. He couldn't imagine not

wearing the red and grey anymore.

He looked out across the field and sighed. His eyes swelled up as he looked out towards the mound. He sat in the dewy grass, imagining he was pitching for West Aurora one more time. He could hear the coaches he had played for in his head, the girls who yelled his name from the bleachers, and his teammates, many of whom he grew up with, telling him to strike out the next batter.

A car drove up and stopped in the parking lot behind him. This caught him off guard. Julio turned and noticed it was his dad.

"May I join you?"

Julio looked at his dad and squinted because of the sun.

"Yeah, nothing's stopping you."

There was a momentary silence.

"How's packing coming? Are the movers very far along?"

"No, son. They have a few more hours to go."

Mr. James sat in the grass and put his arm around his eldest son.

"Listen, I know this is not easy for you. Heck, it's not easy for any of us because we all have friends here, but you'll make friends. As far as baseball goes, you'll get recognized. The school you'll be attending does have a ball team. Not sure how good they are, but they have a team."

There was another pause. Julio was in no mood for small talk. Mr. James stood up. He turned towards the car and stopped.

"You always say 'tough competition is like banging a cast iron -- the harder you bang it, the tougher it gets.' Well son, remember those words. I know it won't be easy for you, but this will make you stronger if you really have the desire."

Even though he heard his dad, Julio was in no mood to respond. He knew his dad was right. He looked around the field one last time. He stood up and headed towards home.

He turned the corner to the street where he lived. The movers were moving boxes out of the house at a pace even Julio was impressed with. He slowed to a walk, tired from his run.

The movers finally emptied the house. Mrs. James called up to the boys who were in their room. "Boys, it's time to go!"

The boys clomped down the stairs. The sound from their feet echoed throughout the house. Each one looked around and notice the house was bare. They looked at each other in amazement.

"Well, I guess it is time for us to roll out?" Julio asked begrudgingly.

She looked at her two sons and sighed. "Yes. It's time for us to go. Take one final look, boys." She stood at the door waiting for them to walk through. Their dad was already in the car waiting patiently. He knew this was not easy for any of them.

Once in the car, Mr. James looked at his wife.

"Well, here we go."

The car remained silent as the family streamed down the interstate towards southern Illinois. The red SUV was packed like a can of sardines with boxes they would immediately need for the house. Their gloves and a ball were among the many goodies.

As they made their way southward, Julio couldn't help but notice the change in scenery. The miles of fields and silos slowly changed to areas of sporadic forests and hills. The drive seemed like an eternity. From Joliet to Marion, the trip took six to seven hours. Julio felt every bit of it.

Jeremy nudged his bigger brother at one point.

"Look over there! Those are big trees!"

They had seen areas like this before, but only in their

travels.

It was nearly eight at night when they passed the city of Marion. Several times they zoomed by signs for the University of Southern Illinois.

Julio's curiosity was peaked.

"Hey dad, just how big is the university we are seeing signs for?"

His dad paused for a moment to reflect.

"I'm not quite sure how big it is. I believe it is one of the larger one's in the state, though."

Julio was instantly curious.

About twenty minutes after they passed Marion, they came to an exit for the town of Franklin. The sun was now below the trees. Julio's jaw dropped when he noticed a dead deer along the side of Highway 15. He had never seen a dead deer along a road before.

Mr. James gripped the steering wheel slightly tighter.

"Look at that boys. A dead deer, not something we see everyday up in Aurora, huh?"

In unison the boys looked at each other.

"Nope."

Ten minutes after exiting the interstate, they reached the small town of Franklin. Along the side of the road was a large Wal-Mart. On the left corner stood a green sign which pointed north towards Carbondale. As they entered Franklin, they noticed a green sign with the population of 3,600 on it and a big wooden sign that stated quite simply, **Welcome to Franklin.**

This certainly had a different feel already than what they were used to. They looked around and noticed only a few fast food restaurants, one which had about four pickups in the parking lot and kids next to them.

They approached the one stop light in town. To their amazement, a female deer stood off to the side of the road. Everyone looked at each other with their mouths open. Mr. James turned left on the street which lead them through the main part of town and away from the deer. They crossed two sets of railroad tracks, passed several old brick stores, one Chinese restaurant, and a pub. They eventually came up to another light with a church on the left. Julio noticed the street was empty except for a few lonely cars. They turned right onto Washington Street. After a few blocks on Washington Street, they came upon a two story house painted white with a porch in the front. The yard was much smaller -- something both boys immediately thought to be advantageous since they were the ones who often were told to mow the lawn.

Julio looked at Jeremy.

"I guess we won't have as much lawn to mow."

Both chuckled, trying to find something funny from their moving experience.

The car came to a halt. Mr. James looked throughout the car. He was exhausted from the drive.

"Well guys, we're here. Let's go inside."

As they got out of the car, Mr. James looked at Julio.

"I thought later in the week we'd drive over to the school and take a look at the field. What do you think?"

Julio, though tired, was able to muster up a smile.

"Can we go tomorrow?"

"Can I go also?" Jeremy curiously chimed.

Julio laughed and playfully punched Jeremy on the shoulder. "Of course, you idiot."

5

Mid July

Mike Williams

Julio, Jeremy and their dad looked in amazement at the Franklin High School baseball field. Julio couldn't help but smile. The infield grass was nicely cut and the outfield glistened in the sun. On each side of the field sat the dugouts which were made out of brick. Needless to say, we took pride in our field. I'll have to say it was one of the nicest ones around, except for Cartersville's, which was on a whole different level.

Julio pointed to the first base line and tapped Jeremy on the shoulder and smiled.

"Gee, I wonder what the school colors are."

The lower part of the dugouts were in blue while the upper part of each dugout was in white. Though Julio was disappointed the colors weren't red and black like West Aurora's, blue was *doable* he thought.

Their dad pointed into the outfield.

"Look boys! Wooden fences!"

"Man, I've never seen that before!" chimed Julio in amazement.

"Neither have I!" added Jeremy excitedly.

Julio turned and looked at the bleachers.

"For a small town, they sure have a good amount of bleachers. Geeze!"

Julio looked into the outfield.

"Dad, what are those white circles out there?"

Mr. James squinted because of the sun.

"Look, there's two in left and four in right," added Jeremy.

"Well, I'll be. It looks like we've moved to a town which has won the State Championship in the past, boys."

All three stood in awe as they silently stared at the signs which were painted to look like baseballs.

Illinois State Champs: 1986

Illinois State Champs: 1988

Regional Champs: 1986

Regional Champs: 1988

Regional Champs: 2006

Regional Champs: 2008

Julio looked at his dad.

"Did you know about this?"

Mr. James looked into the outfield and then at his boys.

"I wish I did!"

Moments after they noticed the signs, the three turned and looked back towards the parking lot. They heard a truck rumble up to the field from a distance away. The field was built on a hill, so at first they did not see the truck. Behind the pickup truck was a cloud of smoke. The truck came up over the slope and slowed to a stop ten feet in front of them.

The pickup was beat up, brown stripped, and dusty with a confederate sticker on the front driver's side door. All three seemed to notice the sticker at the same time.

Julio's dad mumbled to the boys, "No worries. Just be quiet and let me do the talking." The boys stood frozen, unsure what to say or do. They were glad their dad was there with them.

The truck doors popped open on each side and out came two men in their early twenties. The driver was tall and slim with a bulge of tobacco in his mouth. He was wearing a green hat, jeans, and a plaid shirt. The passenger was wearing jeans and a Franklin ball cap along with a blue t-shirt.

The driver slowly walked towards the three. He stopped in front of the pickup, coughed, and looked at his friend for a moment. The gravel crunched underneath the young man's boots as he walked.

"What are you Coons doing here at this field?" the driver said in a stern voice with a slight twang.

Mr. James looked him in the eyes.

"Well, this year my boys are going to attend Franklin High School and we wanted to take a look at the ball field."

"Did you say your boys are going to attend school here?" the driver responded sarcastically looking at his friend. "Coons don't go to this school. You must be thinking of the school down in Clariton. That's where the Coons hang," the young man said while laughing.

"No sir, they're attending Franklin High," Mr. James reiterated.

While the exchange took place, both Julio and Jeremy shook nervously. They had never been addressed in this fashion. Each slowly stepped back behind their dad, afraid of the two strangers.

"Well, you seem like a smart Coon, so let me just tell you something," the passenger muttered in a deep twangy voice, "people like you aren't welcome here in these parts. Just a little advice for yah. You can take it or leave it, but I would take it if I were you."

The two strangers loaded themselves back into the

pickup and headed back down the way they came. Julio's dad looked at Julio first and then Jeremy. Jeremy was looking down and was visibly embarrassed.

Mr. James looked at Julio. "Are you guys okay?"

Julio and Jeremy, had never heard those words in their lives, except in the movies. They definitely didn't expect to hear those words on that day. Julio looked around but not at his dad. His mouth quivered in anger.

Finally after a pause he began walking towards the car. "Let's just get out of here."

When they arrived home, mom stood at the door. She was excited to hear about their adventures.

"How was it guys?"

Julio looked at his mom, then looked back towards his dad, who was still in the driveway. "Ask dad, he'll tell you."

Julio walked through the kitchen and up the stairs to unpack his things from the move.

Two hours later Jeremy walked into the room and sat down on the bed. He was embarrassed, angry, and as scared as his brother. Jeremy always had a little chip on his shoulder. It may have been because he was the youngest of the two and always compared to his brother, or maybe because he was the one who was picked on the most because he was the "little one."

He sat on the bed and looked around the room. Jeremy was anxious to get out of the house.

"Julio, I noticed a park down the street, you wanna go throw?"

"Let me ask you something, Jer. Let's imagine we go to the park and some white guys drive up and get out to bully or threaten us. We won't have dad out there. What in the hell do you think you'll do at that point?! Run? You're an idiot."

"Well maybe so, Julio. But you know it and I know it, we need to get out of the house and we need to throw some. I say we do it. You're supposed to be the big brother here, but all I see is a big sorry ass chicken. I was scared to death out there, but I'll not let them beat me." His voice grew louder with intensity. "Step up, that's all I have to say. Let's beat these guys like you have done to some of the best batters."

Jeremy picked up Julio's glove, threw it at him, and walked out of the bedroom muttering to himself.

Julio sat quietly on his bed. He stood up and followed his brother down the steps of the house. Though Julio had no desire to get out of the house, he knew his brother was right. In tandem, they worked their way to the park with smiles on their faces.

After they threw for an hour, Julio and Jeremy were tired and soaked with sweat.

"Did you notice that ice cream place, Jeremy?"

"Um, yeah. I did, but I don't have any money."

Julio smiled. "I do."

He held up a ten dollar bill his dad had given him as he headed out the door.

"I mean, if we're going to walk twenty minutes we may as well enjoy some ice cream. Right?"

"Sounds good to me!"

Jeremy was never the type to turn down ice cream.

As they made their way towards the ice cream store a red mustang headed their way. Julio immediately noticed the car with three girls in it. The driver had beautiful blonde hair which mesmerized Julio. To their surprise, the young lady honked her car horn as she passed them. Jeremy and Julio smiled at the instant excitement. They quickly forgot about the female fan as they approached the ice cream shop. They both ordered some ice cream and quickly walked out of the store and headed home.

Jeremy looked curiously at his brother.

"Do you think we will have any trouble making the baseball team down here?"

"Jeremy, why would that even cross your mind? Come March, this town won't know what hit them."

6

Mid August

Mike Williams

Summer finally came to an end. Like most schools in the state, Franklin High School went back to school the third week in August. I had no desire to go to school but I had no choice in the matter.

Julio woke up the morning of his first day of school. He didn't want to admit it to Jeremy but he was anxious. I would have been anxious as well if I would've had to attend a new school. Thankfully, I never did. Franklin was all I had known up to this point in my life. Like Julio, Jeremy was a bit nervous. He was afraid he wouldn't be able to find new friends.

After they ate breakfast, Julio and Jeremy made their way to their new school. The parking lot bustled with teenagers. While the two sat in their car, Julio heard the car radio boom country music directly behind him. He looked in his rear view mirror and noticed the red Mustang he had seen several weeks before. Alexa did her best to lip sync as the music blared from the radio. Julio could tell she didn't know half the words but that didn't seem to bother her one bit.

With a pair of round sunglasses on her face, Alexa didn't sit much higher than the steering wheel. Julio smiled.

He looked at Jeremy. "Looks like we have Miss Diva behind us."

The line of cars began to slowly move, which allowed Julio to roll into a parking space. As the two brothers worked their way out of the car, they both noticed several students on the back of their pickups which blared country music.

"Well Jer, you're now in high school." Julio said proudly.

Jeremy smiled. He glanced around the parking lot. "Are we the only African-Americans at this school? Damn!"

Julio noticed the same thing but Jeremy asked the question quicker.

They took several steps towards the school when they both heard a voice from behind.

"Looks like some coons got lost," a voice said with a drawl to it.

The others in the crowd laughed. I was sadly in the crowd, and though I laughed, I didn't know any better.

"Yeah, coons," another one said quietly.

"The last thing we need here at Franklin High School are some blackies," another mumbled. I looked at the guys I was with. I was slightly embarrassed but I didn't tell them to be quiet. When I look back, I can only imagine how Julio and Jeremy felt. The jerks were just loud mouths and full of dumb bluster.

Julio looked at Jeremy. "Just ignore them."

Speechless, Jeremy looked at his brother.

"I'm serious. Don't look back. Just keep walking and ignore them."

Finally for them, the two reached the school doors.

As they entered the main doors of the school Julio looked around nervously. "Jeremy, you'll be okay trust me."

A tear started to form in Jeremy's eye.

"Look at your schedule and go to your first class and stick to the routine. Just like catching in baseball. Stick to the schedule and you'll be okay."

Jeremy, appreciative of his brother's support, wiped his eyes and went on to his first class terrified but excited.

Julio sighed.

As he walked to class, the students around him greeted each other and caught up on the past events of the summer. He heard voices from several of the students. A few girls stared at him disappointingly. "To bad he's black," one muttered.

Blue and white marked the halls. The words **Wildcat Country** hung on each side of the main hall in big blue print with a wildcat painted next to the **Y** in **Country.**

He walked towards his first class which was U.S. History. He climbed up a set of stairs and followed the hall all the way to the end. His first period class was on the left. He felt as if the students stared right through him. Like he didn't exist. Others looked at him like he didn't belong, which, of course, we didn't believe he did. Julio didn't look down. He more than likely didn't want to show any signs of weakness.

He looked to his right and noticed a few girls who were staring coldly at him. "You can take a picture if you want, I'm not going anywhere," he muttered.

The two girls' dropped their mouths. They were speechless! None of the other students had walked into the room yet, so Julio walked up to his teacher and introduced himself.

The teacher, Mr. Wilkins, was a younger teacher with a slight country twang like so many in the community. He was actually a pretty good teacher and also well liked, but his tiresome lectures were tough to sit through in retrospect.

The bell rang and the students began to file into the room. Julio did his best to remain unnoticed. He was trying to do the impossible. Already tired of the jabs directed his way, he sat in the back of the room. Actually, he had heard enough to last him the whole year much less the rest of the day.

The students filed into the room in packs except for a few lone stragglers. After a few minutes Alexa walked through the classroom door. Julio watched her glide across the room.

She was about 5' 4" with long blond hair, big blue eyes, with a fairly athletic built. Alexa was one of those girls most people liked. To her credit, she was always happy or at least seemed to be.

Heck, I'll never forget the first day I met her. I was cluelessly sitting in my social studies class when she walked in. She was new to the school, so needless to say, she stuck out like a sore thumb. A very pretty sore thumb. She walked in and sat down in the desk in front of me. I immediately had butterflies in my stomach. Alexa turned and smiled.

"Hey, what's your name?" she asked me curiously.

"M... M... Mike," I stuttered nervously. I never did have

much game with the ladies, especially when I was in junior high.

"Well Mike, it's nice to meet you. My name is Alexa."

Eventually the fragrance she had on drifted my way. Boy did she smell amazing. Ever since that day Alexa had a way of making my day. Heck, I knew she was never interested in me. But that never mattered. It was Alexa we're talking about.

As she made her way to her seat Julio couldn't take his eyes off of the heeled blonde. From across the room I watched Julio follow her with his eyes. The day definitely looked up as far as Julio was concerned. He didn't seem to care if he stared or not. Heck, she was the one who yelled at him from her car he justified. As he followed her to her seat with his eyes, he noticed a student directly in front of him.

"What's your name?" he asked curiously.

Surprised someone actually asked for his name, Julio smiled. "Julio, what's yours?"

"Mine is Jake. It's nice to meet you." He paused. "Let me just give you a piece of advice dude. I'm not trying to start anything but around here blacks and whites don't go together, so you can look at Alexa all you want but...."

Julio stopped him with a motion of his hand. "Thanks Jake, but I was just admiring the beauty." He smiled. "I do appreciate the hello though."

Jake smiled back, "Not a problem, I guess it's time to learn about history. Whoopdee Doo." Jake turned around twirling his index finger in the air.

The next few periods went by without a hitch. Many of us were in the same classes. To Julio it must have been strange but we didn't know any different.

Alexa was in his first three classes. I know this because I was as well. Alot of us had the same classes together. At one point Alexa glanced at Julio and smiled. Playfully she rolled her eyes as if the teacher's lecture was boring her. I noticed her interaction but since I was oblivious to the world I really didn't think she was flirting with him nor did I think she would be flirting with him since he was black.

"Hey Mike, who's the new guy?"

"What? The black guy? I don't know and I don't really care," I responded.

Alexa looked at me. "Huh." She turned around and didn't talk to me the rest of the period.

Alexa was originally from Southern California, but her parents moved to Southern Illinois during her seventh grade year because of the promotion her dad had received. He became the department chair in the history department at Southern Illinois University which was located in Carbondale. Though she was quite smart, Alexa also knew how to play the game with us guys. Heck she held us in her pinky to be quite honest, thankfully she was pretty genuine. She also recognized the racial prejudice which existed in our town. When she moved to the area she couldn't believe how we viewed minorities, especially since some of her best friends in California were minorities, but to fit in she never brought it up.

Finally the bell rang which ended English. Julio now had to venture to Chemistry. It would've been one of my least favorite classes if it wasn't for our teacher, Coach Wilson. Julio walked into what seemed to be Baseball heaven. He stopped in the middle of the door, which caused Alexa to bump into him. In turn, Alexa's face turned bright red with embarrassment. Alexa laughed and apologized. She quickly walked around Julio all the while biting her lip.

He quickly forgot about his crush as he looked around the room. He looked at his schedule, *Chemistry* but yet the teacher obviously loved sports, especially baseball, and the only thing on the walls science related was the periodic table. Yep! The Chemistry teacher was actually the head baseball coach.

The bell rang and Coach Wilson introduced himself to the class. Julio's eyes darted from wall to wall, picture to picture. Pictures of some of Coach's favorite players hung from the walls. Quotes from Hall of Famers like Yogi Berra and Nolan Ryan were smattered around the room as well.

The end of the school day finally arrived. Julio met his brother where they agreed to meet which was near the front office.

"Follow me Jer."

"Why, where are we going," Jeremy asked curiously.

"Don't ask so many questions. C'mon."

Jeremy begrudgingly followed his brother. He had no desire to stay in the building any longer than he had to but Julio had the car keys.

Most of the students rushed out the door towards the parking lot. Julio and Jeremy headed in the opposite direction like two salmon against the river current.

They arrived at the door to Coach Wilson's room. Julio stopped and took a deep breath. He looked at Jeremy sternly. "Let me do all the talking."

Jeremy nodded his head.

With Julio in the lead, they walked into the room. The wooden floor creaked every few steps Julio and Jeremy took. Coach Wilson fiddled at his desk as if he was hard at work.

"Hello Coach, I wanted to introduce myself. My name is Julio James." Julio confidently stuck out his hand.

Coach looked confused for a moment. "Yeah, I recognize you."

Coach Wilson paused. "So who's this, your brother?"

Julio smiled proudly. "Yes sir, this is my brother, Jeremy."

"What can I do for you?"

"Well sir, I noticed you are the baseball coach and I wanted to take a moment to say hello. My brother and I love the game and we look forward to playing here."

Coach walked over and closed the classroom door. He walked back to his desk and motioned the two young men to sit down. Julio didn't know whether to sit or stand he was so nervous.

"Truth be told, I received a call this summer from a coach up in West Aurora by the name of Coach Shumaker. Do you know him?"

"Yes sir, I played for him the last two years at West

Aurora," Julio replied.

"Well that's what he told me," Coach paused momentarily. "I'm glad you came by. I've been wanting to say hello. What positions do you two play?"

"Well I pitch and play right, and Jeremy catches." Julio replied with pride.

"Awesome, well we can always use some pitching." He looked at Jeremy. "Good catchers are always tough to come by as well," he added with a smile.

Both Julio and Jeremy smiled, appreciative of the warm welcome.

"Thanks for your time Mr. Wilson. I'll see you in class tomorrow."

Coach Wilson reached out with his hand. He firmly grabbed Julio's hand, then Jeremy's.

Julio and Jeremy were excited as they made their way down the stairs towards the main doors of the school. They grinned and pushed each other playfully as they walked towards the car.

Jeremy stopped in his steps fifteen feet from the car. Julio, who was playing with his brother noticed Jeremy's expression. Julio stopped and looked ahead. His jaw dropped as anger rushed through him like a lightning bolt.

Get Out Of Here Coon was painted on the back window in black paint.

"Get in the car, Jer" he said sternly.

In disbelief, Jeremy didn't move. "damnit, get in the car, now!" Julio exclaimed.

Jeremy quickly moved towards the passenger side. The excitement Julio felt ten minutes before had quickly disappeared.

Julio quickly turned on the ignition and drove out of the parking lot. Julio's lips quivered in anger.

Julio pulled into the driveway of his house.

Their mom was by the back door. She was excited to see her two sons. As they walked into the house she glanced their way. "Hey boys, how was school today? Julio did you have a good first day?"

Julio stood by the kitchen door and looked at his mom unhappily. Jeremy was sure his brother would explode but Julio remained eerily quiet. Julio looked at Jeremy and then his mom.

"How was my day?" He asked rhetorically. "Go outside and look at the car and see for yourself." Angrily, Julio turned and left the kitchen.

Their mom quickly walked outside.

Jeremy found himself in the kitchen by himself. He threw his arms up in the air. He looked around and decided to get a glass of milk.

Jeremy finished off the glass of milk and two cookies. He looked at the time and realized it had been awhile since he had heard from his mom. It was too quiet for him. He stood up and made his way outside. To his surprise his mom was busily cleaning up the windows.

She looked at her son and flashed a half hearted smile as she continued to wash the window. "I take it you had this on your car window this afternoon, huh son?"

"Yep mom it was there." Jeremy responded looking around, but not at mom.

"Do you want us to tell the principal?"

"No mam."

"Other than this how was your day?" She asked as she worked to clean up the car.

He shrugged his shoulders and tried to act as if everything was okay. "Yeah things were good. We got to meet the head coach today. Typical day otherwise I guess."

"Well son, it'll get better."

After nearly thirty-five minutes their mom came inside and yelled for Julio. "Julio, get your butt down here."

Julio rounded the corner of the stairs and walked into the kitchen. "Yeah?"

She was in the process of organizing the table for dinner when Julio walked in. "The car is taken care of, and I am sorry it happened. Other than that how was your day?"

Julio looked at his mom. He was in disbelief she had taken the paint off the windows. He shrugged his shoulders.

"Talk to me, I want to know how your day was." She reiterated.

"The day was okay. Can we not talk right now?"

She turned away. "Okay, but if you ever feel like talking we're here." She turned back towards Julio only to notice he had gone back upstairs.

7

Mid August

Mike Williams

The next morning came way too soon. Julio quietly put on some sweats and sauntered to the basement to work out. Julio was glad to be able to clear his mind as he ran on the treadmill and lifted weights.

Eventually Jeremy joined his brother in the basement. He was still not fully awake.

As Jeremy yawned he felt a SMACK on his butt! "Uggg!" Jeremy yelled in pain.

Julio laughed. "I'd like to see what you're going to do about that bro!"

Jeremy didn't see the humor. He gave his brother a death stare or at least tried to. It didn't affect Julio very much.

Julio winked at his brother. "Are we going to have a better day?"

Jeremy grinned. "I thought it was pretty cool coach knew who we were."

"Yeah, that was pretty awesome. I was actually surprised. I have to say the girls at this school aren't bad looking either." Julio leaned back on the bench with dumbbells in each hand.

Eventually Julio went upstairs to wash up as 6 O'clock approached. He was determined to like Franklin High School.

As they drove into the school parking lot, they could feel numerous sets of eyes pierce through them. Country music blared in the background from one of the pickups. Julio and Jeremy pulled into a parking space and worked their way out of the car.

"Hey boy!" Zach yelled. In case you are wondering, Zach was one of the better athletes in the school. Like Julio and I, he was a junior. He also was similar to many of the others from Franklin...a redneck with little desire to know anyone of color.

Julio and Jeremy ignored Zach, so he yelled at them again. "I said hey boy!"

Julio looked at Zach, I, and the others who were on the bed of the pickup. He glanced at Zach with a devilish grin. "Well, son, I'm not sure who you're talking to, but from the looks of your size, you're the boy," Julio paused. "When you grow six inches and, I'd say, about sixty pounds, then come to me and you'll be free to call me boy."

Julio turned away. I couldn't believe it! I even nudged one of the other guys playfully. Julio got Zach good.

Pissed, Zach looked at me. "What are you smiling at jagoff?"

Needless to say his jagoff comment kind if pissed me off. "Oh nothing, I'm just curious if you're going to let him get the best of you...Idiot."

Zach looked at me and grunted. He knew Julio had gotten the best of him.

Julio stopped and turned towards the group. Zach jumped down from his pickup and took a step towards Julio.

"One more thing. Next time you paint my car can you use blue and white. I mean since it's the school colors and all."

Zach's jaw dropped in disbelief. He looked at me with amazement. Now I have to say, we didn't put the paint on the window but Julio nailed us! *This guy has guts* I thought to myself.

"Dang bro" Jeremy whispered, "your hot today!"

Julio laughed, "Yeah it was that smack on your butt that got me going!"

The rest of the day seemed to breeze by uneventfully.

Throughout the day students would glance at him unpleasantly but Julio did his best to ignore them. Every class Alexa was in made it all worthwhile.

Outside of his room, Coach Wilson was in the middle of a conversation with Zach when Julio approached the door.

"Julio, I want you to meet one of the juniors who has played for me since his freshman year. This is Zach."

Julio grinned. He reached out to shake Zach's hand. Zach, looked at Julio in disbelief. I wish I could've seen it!

Julio smiled, "yeah, Coach, we met earlier today," and quickly sat down after shaking Zach's hand.

The rest of the day sailed by without any issues. The bell rang and another day was done. Julio and Jeremy walked towards their car, which they agreed to do every day together until they felt safe. They both expected the worst. But today there was nothing on the car.

Julio took a breath. "Well bro, looks like there's nothing on the car today, let's get home and throw some."

8

Early September

Mike Williams

A few weeks had passed. Signs were hung in the halls in support of the football team. Up and down the streets of Franklin one could see banners encouraging the Wildcats. Like their baseball team, Franklin always seemed to have a competitive football team. The biggest rival in football was always Carbondale, a larger town north of Franklin where the University was founded.

Overall, Julio enjoyed his classes and most of the teachers. Though they were always close, Jeremy and Julio seemed to gravitate towards each other more and more.

The Friday morning of our first home football game Jake turned around in their first period class. Jake would often make conversation with Julio about classes, football, and the playoff race in baseball. Jake was a huge Cardinals fan as were most of us since Southern Illinois had a huge Cardinals fan base because our close proximity to St. Louis. From time to time he would jab Julio because he was a Cubs fan.

"Are you going to the game tonight?"

Unsure, Julio shrugged his shoulders.

"Well it's bound to be a good game. I recommend you come out, it's always fun," Jake said with a smile. Though it seemed like an invite, Julio knew better.

Moments before the first period bell rang, Alexa scampered into class. Far from being the school trouble maker, Alexa always found a way to work her way out of trouble. Heck, I think she could've talked her way out of a prison sentence even with the toughest judge. Some of the girls hated her for it but the majority of the students and teachers liked her because she was pretty genuine.

Alexa slid to the back of the room next to Julio and plopped down. She looked at him and smiled.

I for one thought she looked incredible in her denim jeans and blue football jersey which said *Wildcats* across the front. She had a pair of blue heels on as well which was pretty standard for her. Julio couldn't take his eyes off her no matter how hard he tried. She noticed him stare at her several times. She couldn't help but giggle to herself. He tried to talk to her but he couldn't muster up the courage.

The teacher droned on and on about the Louisiana Purchase or something like that. I can't remember I was so bored. Alexa leaned over and dropped a piece of folded paper on the ground. She looked at Julio, then up front, and then back towards Julio. Julio looked at the piece of paper and then Alexa. Confused, he looked back down at the folded piece of paper. She rolled her eyes, smiled, and leaned down to pick up the paper which was in the aisle between them. She gently put it on Julio's desk.

He looked at her in disbelief. Was this girl hitting on him? The lucky son of a gun! He opened up the note and smiled.

Hey my name is Alexa, I'm sure you knew that by now but if not, hello. I've been wanting to say hello to you for some time. People around here can be mean to outsiders so don't let it get you down. I was an outsider at one point.

P.S. you know that was me honking at you this summer right?

He looked at her and mouthed *thank you* followed by a huge grin. He put the note up to his nose and smelled the nicest flowery fragrance one could imagine.

Alexa sat up and smiled. She flicked her hair over her left shoulder and looked ahead towards the front of the room.

Much to Julio's disappointment, first period came to a close. The bell rang and they stood up to leave for their next class. Julio muttered to Alexa sarcastically, "that was quite a lesson."

Jake turned around with a look of disbelief. He had no idea Alexa gave Julio a note. Julio walked out of the room followed by Alexa who was a few students behind him. Julio didn't want to ruin the moment or push it. He headed towards his the next class, the whole time he wore a big grin on his face.

The rest of the day went by fast. It didn't hurt Alexa gave him a note. Finally, the school day came to a close and the weekend was here. He and Jeremy walked towards their car with another week of school down.

"Hey Jer, would you be interested in going to the football game tonight?"

Half surprised, Jeremy pondered Julio's question. "Sure, why not? We can scope out the girls from the other school since we can't date any from here." They both laughed at the sad state of affairs which existed here in Franklin.

They approached the football field. The sun was about to lower below the horizon. The game was not for another half hour but the parking was already a bear. This caught Julio and Jeremy off guard. They finally gave up and parked near the exit of the parking lot. There weren't many activity choices in Franklin, which is why the games were always packed.

The walk into the stadium took a couple of minutes but they didn't seem to care. It was a nice evening. Julio often went to the games when he attended West Aurora but the community wasn't as closely knit. Rarely did the crowds get very big unless it was the playoffs or they faced one of their rivals like East Aurora.

The stadium was built at the bottom of a hill in a bowl shape. On all sides of the stadium there were trees, except for the nearest entrance where they entered the stadium. The blue and white school colors were everywhere -- on the gate, the midfield, and the end zone. Every five yards the numbers were either blue or white starting at the goal line. The word *Wildcat* was painted in both of the end zones and midfield.

Jeremy could not believe his eyes. "Bro, there's crowd here, what is up with that?!"

Julio looked at Jeremy, "I guess people around here don't have as much to do, huh?"

Many of the people had blue or white on. Julio slapped Jeremy on the side. "Next time... remind me to wear blue."

A few minutes passed.

Jeremy poked Julio. "Is it me or are we the only two African-Americans?"

"Yep, I think we are. Aren't we the special ones."

As they worked their way up the bleachers, Julio noticed Alexa who was on the track because she was on the cheerleading squad. He noticed her look his way. They both timidly waved at each other and smiled.

Nicole, one of the other cheerleaders and a friend of Alexa, noticed the exchange between the two. She leaned in Alexa's direction. "Did you just wave at him?"

Alexa looked at her. "Yeah. Why?"

"Well he's black, duh."

"And I guess that's to keep me from being friendly towards him?" Alexa snapped back.

"Well, just don't get too friendly with him, that's gross." Nicole sternly replied.

Alexa looked at her for a moment in disbelief. Alexa dropped the whole conversation even though Nicole's opinions bothered her.

The evening went on without any problems for Julio and Jeremy. They enjoyed the game and thought Franklin, especially for its size, played really good football.

Julio noticed Zach play. He was one of the best athletes on the field in all actuality. Several colleges in the area had been in the process of recruiting him.

The game was nearing the end when a couple of guys approached Julio and Jeremy. Both of them were in blue t-shirts and jeans. The taller of the two had a slender built with disheveled hair. The other one was short and stocky and was rough shaven with a short haircut. Julio noticed a wad of chew in the side of his cheek, which didn't help his appearance in Julio's eyes.

The taller of the two stepped closer to the Julio and Jeremy. "What the hell are you two doing on this side of the field?"

Julio was slightly confused or at least pretended to be. "Do I know you? Do you go to Franklin?"

The two strangers laughed. The tallest one stuck out his index finger and pointed at Jeremy and Julio. "No, we don't. We graduated last year punk."

"Well then I guess things have changed in a year, my man," Julio replied with smile. "Listen, my brother and I are just trying to enjoy the game."

Julio looked at the older couple who sat next to them throughout the game. "They could vouch I'm sure. We haven't been loud or disruptive. If we were loud I'm sure they would've said something three and half quarters ago. So will you please just let us enjoy the rest of the game?"

An older man who was sitting next to Julio and Jeremy looked at the two agitators. "Look, these two young men have been fine, so will you please let us enjoy the rest of the game? You're blocking the field."

Humored, Jeremy nudged Julio with his foot.

The two strangers walked away irritated and defeated.

Once they walked away, the oldest gentleman looked at Julio and Jeremy. "Look boys, African-Americans are generally not welcomed in this town so you need to expect people like that to come up to you. Not everyone is like that though. Welcome to Franklin."

As the game drew to a close, Julio and Jeremy decided to leave. They both held their breath as they neared their car. To their glee, nothing was written on it. They both sat down in the car and breathed a sigh of relief.

9

Mid October

Mike Williams

As the semester continued, Julio became more comfortable with the school and the students around him. He still didn't feel welcomed by most of the students, but he had come to accept it. Julio figured it would be just a matter of time before some of us accepted him, and if we never did, he didn't want anything to do with us.

The air began to cool and leaves slowly began to change colors. I always looked forward to the Franklin falls because the colors were always pretty cool. Julio could tell southern Illinois was slightly warmer.

Julio and Jeremy drove up to the school after another exciting Franklin weekend. We were all excited because Franklin High had won the previous Friday to remain undefeated for the season with just a few games left. The team had also qualified for the state playoffs. Of course Zach had a great game. He rushed and passed for over 200 yards.

No longer had Julio and Jeremy received the jeers like they had at the beginning of the year. Some students would give them the stink eye from time to time but rarely were the comments made to them like in the beginning of the year. A few curious students would ask Julio about his baseball experience. Sadly, the times I sat next to him I never asked him questions. I guess I wasn't really that concerned.

Even though Julio knew a few colleges were interested in him he didn't feel it was necessary to mention it to any of us. I guess he felt his play would speak for itself in the spring.

Sometimes Jeremy wanted to tell the other students how good his brother was, but he thought better of it when Julio threatened to "beat the tar out of him" if he said a word. Jeremy knew Julio did not give his brother idle threats. He meant what he said.

Julio went into his first period class and sat in his normal spot. By now Julio, like a lot of us, wore sleeves to school because the temperatures began to drop consistently into the 50s and 60s during the day. The building must have been older than Abraham Lincoln. Some days the heat blasted from the radiators and it felt like you were in a sauna while other days we felt like we were in the middle of Antarctica because the radiators didn't run. There was no rhyme or reason for the room temperatures. Needless to say, getting dressed each day for school was always an interesting endeavor.

From time to time Alexa would sit near Julio, but most times she sat across the room. She always made it a point to look his way and roll her eyes while Mr. Wilkins talked though. Jake sat in the same spot every day which humored Julio. He wondered if Jake didn't have any friends in class. Did he feel sorry for Julio, or did he just have no desire to move since that was where he had sat since the first day? Who was he to question the habits of another student he finally determined. He always sat in the same spot as well.

Alexa came into the room and walked to the far side. He noticed her walk in because she looked incredible in her pink sweater, jeans, and boots. He couldn't take his eyes off her. She definitely knew how to stand out, like a rose in the desert.

To his surprise, she sat directly behind him. He didn't know if he should be excited or nervous. In front of him sat Jake who seemed to watch him like a hawk, and behind him was the girl Julio had the biggest crush on in his three years of high school. What a predicament huh?

Julio tried to play it cool. As the minutes passed he felt

repeated kicks on the back of his seat. She stopped tapping her boots when Mr. Wilkins called on her.

"Alexa, who was the President from Tennessee?"

Alexa laughed and threw her hands in the air. "I don't have a freaken clue sir." To be honest I didn't have a clue either.

"Julio, can you assist Alexa, since she doesn't have a freaken clue?"

"Yes sir, it was Andrew Jackson."

"Smarty farty..." Alexa muttered.

Julio grinned.

The class period continued on without much excitement for the next thirty minutes except for the occasional tap by Alexa's boots on the bottom of Julio's seat. Julio felt a tug on his right side next to the wall. He looked down and noticed a piece of paper on the ground.

He reached down and picked up the paper. He couldn't help but notice it was a piece of pink paper which matched Alexa's sweater and it smelled like flowers like the previous note. He was slightly nervous as he opened the letter, but he was extremely excited since he liked her. Besides, any note with perfume on it was probably not a hate letter.

Julio quietly opened up the note, but knew he had to

be sneaky about doing so. Mr. Wilkins was known to take the notes and read them in front of the class. Already this year he had read five notes from our class alone and Julio surely did not want to be number six.

Hey Julio, I just wanted to say hello.

Julio grinned with pride.

After science class, Julio left the room and stopped at the water fountain. He felt the presence of someone next to him. It was Nicole, Alexa's friend.

"Excuse me, is your name Julio?" she asked with an attitude.

Next to Nicole were a few of her friends.

"Yes it is, your Nicole right? Alexa's friend?" Julio responded with a slight smile. He hoped this would be a friendly hello, but he could tell by the way she was standing it wasn't going to be.

"Well who I am is NOT important and none of your business. What is my business is Alexa and you. She's white, you're NOT, so I'd suggest you stay away from her. Understand?" Nicole said this as she sternly pointed her finger at Julio.

Confused, Julio looked at Nicole for a few seconds. Heck, I remember when I sauntered by the fountain. I actually felt sorry for the guy. I mean, the guy was just at the water fountain for a drink and Nicole had to get all huffy with him. I mean, geeze!

Julio gave Nicole a smirk. "I have no clue what you're talking about. Can you fill me in?"

"Well again, I'm just saying what is best for her. I have no concern for you. She's my friend, so stay away from her. I don't even know why your here. You're black. Do you see any other blacks in this school?" She moved her hands towards the rest of the student body who walked by. "No, you don't, which means you don't belong here. Since you don't belong here, fitting in isn't possible."

Julio was in no mood to have his day ruined so he began to walk away.

"Just where do you think you're going!?"

Julio looked at her and smiled. "Look Nicole -- your name is Nicole so that's how I'm going to address you -- I have no desire to waste my time right now with you, so I'm just going to walk away. Besides, I thought you didn't want me to talk to anyone, and I assume that includes you."

He turned to walk away.

Nicole wasn't used to guys walking away from her, so she grunted and stomped her foot forcibly.

"Get the hell out of here!" she yelled.

She looked for support from her friends. When she didn't get the desired response from Julio or her friends she stomped to her next class.

By the end of the day he felt defeated. Nicole's outburst had gotten to him. He wasn't sure if going after Alexa would be worth it.

Julio stopped in his tracks as Jeremy and Julio made their way to the car. "Jeremy, I hate to do this, but I want to talk to coach for a moment."

Jeremy didn't answer.

"Come on up and you can wait in the hall, it won't be long, besides I don't want you waiting by yourself out here.

"Sure, I have no problem waiting," Jeremy responded lying through his teeth.

They walked back into the building and up to Coach Wilson's room. Julio knocked nervously on the side of the door. Coach looked up and smiled. "What can I do for you?"

"Can I close the door, Coach?"

"Sure, go ahead."

Julio walked into the room. He closed the door behind him and approached the front desk. Jeremy waited for him in the hall.

"What brings you in here this afternoon?"

Julio cleared his throat. "Well coach, I have a serious question for yah. Well, really two. First off, there's a girl here at school who I think likes me." He paused as he re-positioned himself. "Well, today someone told me to stay away from her. What should I do?"

Coach looked at him and smiled. "What do you mean 'what should you do'? Go after her! Alexa is an open minded, smart, intelligent girl. Something you won't find often around here."

Julio's jaw dropped. "How did you know it's her?"

Coach smiled, "Don't you worry about that. I'm correct, right?"

"Yes sir, you are."

"Okay, the fact I'm right is all that matters. She's smart, well grounded, and her parents aren't your typical people like most around here."

Confused, Julio asked, "How so coach?"

"Well, they're originally from California, and her dad is a professor at the university in Carbondale. So the question you have to ask yourself is -- is she worth the trouble? I know the answer. You have to determine it on your own."

"Thanks coach, I appreciate your time."

"So what's the last question for me?"

"Oh yeah, it's getting cooler outside and Jeremy and I have been throwing some in the park. Is it possible to throw in the gym before or after school this winter?"

Coach smiled. "Let me talk to the basketball coaches and get back to you. I don't see it being an issue. We just need to make sure you're not in the way of the basketball teams when they start up."

"Coach, I'm excited about the season. I appreciate all you've done so far." Julio stuck out his hand for coach to shake.

"Not a problem Julio. I'm happy to assist you and your brother. I have a feeling you will make the team. Now get out of here and take your brother with you."

Julio walked out of the room feeling better about everything.

10

Early November

Mike Williams

Fall had set in at Franklin. The football team just finished one of its best seasons in school history before a loss in the quarterfinals of the state playoffs. Even though Franklin High lost in the quarterfinals the players needed to hold their heads high because of the solid season. Zach had his best season ever but sadly it wasn't enough to carry the team.

Even though chemistry wasn't Julio's favorite subject, he looked forward to class. Mainly because coach taught the class.

Julio walked in and was stopped next to Coach Wilson.

"I suppose you have a catcher?" Coach asked.

"Yep, my brother will catch me if that is okay with you? Can we throw tomorrow after school?"

Coach Wilson paused. He smiled fondly at his young ball player. "The basketball coaches would prefer you throw in the morning."

"That's fine. I just want to throw." Needless to say, Julio was excited.

The next morning was chillier than the previous days as the two walked into the school. Julio and Jeremy made their way into the gym. The gym was totally empty except for the one or two students who had to go to their gym locker for one reason or another. Julio looked at his brother with an excited grin. Jeremy looked around the gym and then back towards Julio.

"Are you ready to catch some smoke?"

Jeremy laughed. "I could catch you in my sleep."

Jeremy threw down his bag of gear and began to unpack his catcher's equipment.

He put on his equipment while Julio stretched. During his freshman year he saw one of the varsity players pull a muscle in his leg because he failed to stretch properly. Ever since that incident, Julio was always afraid he would pull something so he never took stretching lightly.

Even though he wasn't on the team yet, he made sure he wore a blue t-shirt. To him it showed pride in the school and, to be honest, it was something a few of us from the team immediately appreciated whether we wanted to admit or not.

Julio and Jeremy lined up 15 feet from each other. They began to throw and loosen up their arms. One could have heard a pin drop. Every few throws Julio backed up a few more feet. Still not a word was spoken. Before long, the two were standing on the baselines of the basketball court. Each time they caught the ball a loud *pop* echoed throughout the gym.

While they threw, Julio and Jeremy noticed Coach Wilson come in and sit down on the bleachers. Both of them pretended to ignore their future coach.

After several minutes Julio looked at Jeremy and yelled, "I'm ready."

Jeremy squatted into his catching position.

Jeremy widened his glove so as to give Julio a bigger target. Julio went into his motion. He picked up his left leg and kicked it towards Jeremy. The ball hit Jeremy's glove with a less than impressive *pop*.

Coach Wilson's mind slowly wandered, unimpressed with the first few pitches. Me, Zach, and a few others came in and sat near coach. What can I say? We were curious.

Julio threw a few more. Up to this point we were less than impressed. I looked at Zach. "This guy has nothing."

Zach looked at me. "Yeah, I mean he has a decent form but he's going to get rocked."

After ten pitches, Julio apparently decided to turn it up

a notch.

Jeremy looked out of the corner of his eye towards Coach Wilson. Jeremy smiled. "Hey I think you're loose."

Humored, Zach nudged me. I playfully nudged him back.

Julio took a step back. He positioned his feet side by side and went into his motion. He picked his left leg up and kicked his leg towards his brother. He released the ball.

POP!

The ball hit Jeremy's glove which caused Jeremy's hand to sting. "Good pitch, bro."

I sat up and looked at Zach. "Holy shit!" I whispered.

A few seats down Coach Wilson sat up.

He frantically looked at us. "Will you guys get the hell out of here before you get us in trouble! Move your butts!" Just so you know, the rules stated the coach could only be with two players at a time during the off season. We frantically stood up and walked quickly towards the door. I was the first to walk out. Zach was behind me. He stopped to watch Julio pitch one more time.

POP!

The ball hit the glove even louder! Zach looked at Julio unhappily. "Son of a bitch," he mumbled.

It was at that point I realized, whether we liked it or not, Julio was on the team and so was his brother. I looked at Zach. "Get over it, he's going to be on the team."

That was the last thing Zach wanted to hear. He looked at me and scowled.

"Shut the hell up."

After thirty pitches Julio and Jeremy called it quits. Both of them had worked up a sweat. Julio motioned to Jeremy. He was tired and ready to stretch. Disappointed, Jeremy dropped his head and walked towards his brother.

They fell to the floor to stretch. Coach walked over to them. "Guys, good job. Julio, I liked how you looked today." He looked at Jeremy. "Jeremy, I like how you caught him."

He looked at Julio. "Get cleaned up and I'll see you in class, bud."

Coach Wilson walked out of the gym in a rush. If you didn't know any better, you would've thought he had to go to the bathroom. He walked through the gym doors in search of the athletic director, Mike Jones. He had to tell someone about his new ball players.

He passed students in the hall who wanted to say hello, but he was too distracted to talk. Baseball was on his mind. He walked into the office and stopped at the main desk.

"Where the heck is Mike today?!" he exclaimed throwing his arms up in the air.

The secretaries looked at each other and then coach. "Sorry, we haven't seen him yet, can we help you with something, coach?" one of the ladies politely asked.

"Just tell him I need to talk him as soon as possible, please." Coach Wilson turned and rushed out the door and down the hall.

In between first and second periods, Coach Jones came up to Coach Wilson's room. "Did you need to see me?" He asked curiously.

"Yes I did coach. You need to talk to Julio and get the skinny on him and make sure everything is good. He was throwing beebees this morning! Can you do that for me Mike?"

Coach Jones smiled. "Yes, I will find out what you need on him. I'm tellin you though, he's legal to play."

"Lord, I hope your right!" Coach Wilson replied sharply. He looked away for a moment. "I just hope the idiots in this community realize what they have before they chase him away."

11

Mid December

Mike Williams

Like many of us, Jeremy and Julio were ready for their Christmas break. Heck, I know I was. The weeks between Thanksgiving and the end of the semester seemed to fly by, thankfully. Even though they had struggled to make friends, they liked their teachers.

Even though the football and baseball teams were by far our best sports at the school, the basketball team was in the middle of a surprisingly good year. The team was actually competitive unlike other years. Many of us were excited about the game against Carbondale, which was coming up. Banners expressing our support for the team dotted the halls.

The week had been a long one for Julio. Not only were tests coming up in a number of our classes, but he also missed his Aurora friends.

It was Thursday morning and he was barely able to stay awake.

Mr. Wilkins walked to the front of the room as soon as the bell rang. He was about to start talking endlessly about the Civil War when he heard a quiet knock at the door. Frustrated, Mr. Wilkins stopped mid-sentence and looked towards the door. For a variety of reasons, one being his disdain for tardies, he kept his door locked at all times. He especially hated tardy students.

The wooden floors amplified any steps made, especially when Mr. Wilkins walked because he took heavy footsteps. Imagine Frankenstein -- yeah, that was him. He wasn't a very big guy though, oddly enough. For some reason, students were always afraid to get him mad even though he had a great sense of humor. If given the chance, he could have intimidated Mussolini if he wanted to.

Aggravated, he approached the door. His aggravation started to slide when he noticed Alexa. He still opened the door unhappily.

Alexa stood in the doorway grinning from ear to ear. She walked in with a piece of paper in her hand. "Sorry sir," she said smiling innocently.

He looked at the note and then at her and then huffed. What could he say? It was Alexa.

I looked at Zach and shook my head. He smiled and shrugged his shoulders. Likewise, Julio watched the exchange play out. There was a reason she made him nervous. Most of the guys tried to ask her out but she was never interested. She especially disliked the ones she thought had a "backwards" way of thinking.

She quickly moved to the back where Julio was sitting. He tried to act sophisticated and attentive at the same time. Julio wasn't very good at either.

Julio did his best to pay attention to Mr. Wilkins and his incessant droning about the Civil War, but he couldn't help but repeatedly glance towards Alexa. The poor guy couldn't take his eyes off of her and her beautiful blonde hair. If you asked me, I especially loved the curls she always had in her hair.

As the period neared the end, Mr. Wilkins decided to stop and end class early. Lucky us!

Julio looked at Alexa and decided now was the time. "You going to the game tomorrow night?" he asked nervously.

Alexa smiled. "You know... I haven't quite decided, what are you doing? Are you going to the game?"

Julio looked away momentarily. "I've been interested in going to a game, but I've heard the team isn't very good."

Alexa ripped out a piece of paper from her notebook and frantically wrote with her favorite pink pen. He noticed the hearts dotting some of the letters.

She folded the paper and gave it to Julio with a big smile on her face. The timing was impeccable. As soon as she handed him the paper the bell rang. The rest of class, including me, rushed the door like a jailbreak. Not Julio. Not this time. He sat in his desk and waited for Alexa.

He opened up the note and smiled. He loved the hearts which dotted her letters. As he quickly read the note his smile became bigger.

COOL PIZZA PLACE IN CARBONDALE

TOMORROW AT 6:30? HERE'S MY ADDRESS:

23 CRAWFORD WAY,

HUGS!

ALEXA

He looked up and noticed Alexa was still next to her desk. "So what do you think?"

"Yeah, I'd love to."

"Awesome. Well, we need to get to get to class before everyone starts talkin." Alexa replied with a smile. "Call me tonight and we can work out the details."

The rest of the day flew by, as did Friday. He failed to let his parents know he had a date until Friday after school. The sly dog. Julio knew they would drill him with questions.

That was something I always dreaded when I mentioned to my parents I'd be going on a date. "Who's the girl? Tell me about her! Does she play sports? bla bla bla." Yeah, I don't blame him one bit. The thought of his parents asking a lot of questions drove him nuts with embarrassment no matter how much he liked her.

He walked into the house. His dad was still at work while his mom lingered around the house. It always seemed like she was at home awaiting the arrival of her two sons. Of course, she was always busy with what whatever moms do throughout the day.

Julio sat in one of the kitchen chairs. "Hey Mom, do you mind if I go out tonight with a girl from school?"

She turned around. "Who's this girl you're thinking of, son?"

"Oh, it's just a girl I know from school. She's actually from California and moved here a few years ago. She's not like most of the people around here."

"Ohhhh, she's not, huh? Well I trust you, son." She went back to washing dishes. "Be safe though, okay?"

"Yes mam, I will." He tapped his fingers on the table nervously.

"Uh mom, do you have some money?"

She turned around and smiled. "Yeah, you can have some money," She walked into the family room, and a few seconds later she re-appeared with fifty dollars in cash. "Is this going to be enough?"

Julio snatched the cash from her hand as if he was a gunslinger from the Wild West. With a quick thanks he ran upstairs to change cloths.

On the other side of town, Alexa was in her room. She heard a quiet knock at the door. She was always upfront with her parents about the people she dated, especially her mom. They were extremely close which I truly admired. Then again, her mom was super awesome, much like Alexa.

Her mom walked in and sat down on the bed and watched as her daughter prepared for her date with Julio.

"So tell me about this gentleman you are having pizza with tonight. What's his name, sweetie?"

"Oh, I haven't told you his name, have I? His name is Julio and he is African-American."

Alexa could see her mom through the mirror as she put on her makeup. "He's new to Franklin. His family moved here from the Chicago area. Umm, he plays baseball. He can be quiet in class, but he's SUPER nice. The others in school haven't been too nice, which sucks."

"Well, do you think the kids will stop talking to you if you go out with this young man?"

"Mom, his name is Julio. And you know, if others can't take it, then they aren't my friends."

Alexa finished putting on her makeup. She turned around to face her mom. "So how do I look?"

"Sweetie, you look truly amazing. I'm so proud of you."

"Do you think Daddy will have an issue with me going out with Julio?"

She put her arm around Alexa. "Sweetie, as long as he makes you happy, treats you right, and is a gentleman, your dad will support you." She paused. "You know that."

Alexa heard a car pull into the driveway. She frantically looked at her watch. "Oh crap, I lost track of time."

The doorbell rang.

Her dad yelled from the base of the stairs. "Do you want me to get the door?"

Alexa scurried for her purse and boots. She could hear three people laugh in the room below which put her at ease.

She ran her hands through her hair one more time followed by a quick look into the mirror to make sure everything was just right.

Her boot heels clomped down the stairs which caused everyone else to stop.

"Well here she is," her dad said excitedly as he wrapped his arm around her. He proudly looked at his daughter. "Well you two have a good time tonight and be safe. Remember, watch for the deer on your way to and from Carbondale, okay?"

Alexa locked arms with Julio and quickly guided him outside. "Let's get outta here before my dad starts telling you stories," she whispered.

They made their way up the highway towards Carbondale. Since the big move, he had never been out of Franklin.

Near the end of their dinner, Alexa's phone buzzed. She curiously picked up the phone. Alexa's shoulders slumped in disbelief. "Nicole drives me nuts, I love her but dang."

Julio smiled. "Yeah, what's the deal with her? She told me to stay away from you several weeks ago."

Alexa pounded her hands on the table. Her hands hit table so hard, the shakers even rattled! "You have to be kidding me!" She looked away momentarily. "Sometimes I feel like Franklin is stuck in the 1960s!"

"You feel like we are in the 1960s?! Put yourself in my

place."

Alexa sat back in her seat. She looked at him and then looked away. Her smile all but disappeared. "I hate this conversation. Let's get out of here and go home."

Worried he had upset her, Julio put his hand on her wrist. "Thanks for everything. I had fun tonight. You're awesome!"

Alexa smiled shyly. "Thanks, you are pretty awesome too."

While driving back to Franklin, Julio slid his hand down next to her hand and bumped it. Alexa felt the bump and smiled. She opened up her hand so theirs could intertwine.

He was now on top of the world, as was Alexa. They sat quietly, held hands, and smiled the rest of the way home. Life was good.

12

Mid December

Mike Williams

Almost every Sunday afternoon, Nicole, Alexa, and their friend Janet got together to study, talk about boys, and socialize. Both Janet and Nicole were from Franklin, which sometimes made Alexa feel like the outsider even though the three were pretty inseparable.

Janet's parents were one of the richer farming families in the community. Janet always felt a little self-conscience for some reason. I personally thought she was the least pretty of the three and, to be honest, she was my least favorite of the three to be around.

Every spring and fall her dad hired migrant workers. She thought her dad was doing them a service by hiring them to work on their farm. I always thought that was a bit pompous.

Two o'clock approached and Alexa finally pulled into the driveway. While Alexa waited for her hot cocoa, Nicole sipped on hers.

Alexa noticed they had their math books out, so she began to look for her's. Janet clanked in the kitchen as she prepared the hot chocolate for Alexa. Even though the three were friends and pretty inseparable, they would talk about the others behind each other's backs. I always thought it was a bit funny. The activity tired Alexa, even though she thrived on it like the other two. Oh the irony.

Nicole looked into the kitchen. She looked at Alexa curiously. Alexa could feel the barrage of questions that were about to head her way.

"Where were you Friday night? Why didn't you go to the game?" Nicole whispered.

"I was out on a date."

"Nooo way! Who was it? All the hotties were at the game the other night. Was it some hunk from the University?"

"Ewww, nooo!"

Nicole's interest was piqued. "Well who was it then?! It wasn't that black boy you're pretending to like, was it?"

Alexa didn't answer.

"Eww, it was him! You went out with that boy? This is so, like, not cool."

Janet could hear the other two talking, but she couldn't make out what they were talking about. Janet was especially worried she may have missed some juicy gossip, so she hurriedly fixed Alexa's drink. As soon as she finished fixing Alexa's cup of hot chocolate, Janet quickly walked into the room and smiled.

"What are you two bitches talking about?" Janet asked curiously.

"Did you know she went out with that black boy from school?" Nicole chimed.

"What?! You went on a date with that monkey?" Janet blasted. "I can't believe you would stoop to that level. I mean, you could have any white boy in our school!"

"I bet he made you pay, didn't he?" Nicole added.

Alexa sat in her seat and listened to the girls rattle off insults.

"Listen, I came here to study. I knew you two were going to be inquiring about where I was on Friday, which is fine, but let it be. Geeze!"

Nicole looked at Janet then Alexa with a fake smile. "Well, we do have some math to study here. Don't we Janet? We don't want to upset the princess."

Alexa threw down her math book. "I love you both, but you guys can be such jerks sometimes. I'm going home. Good luck on your tests this week and I'll talk to you both later. I mean, you two don't have to like who I date, but you don't have to be rude about it...at least to my face."

She angrily shoved her books into her bag and walked out of the house.

Janet and Nicole were speechless. They never expected Alexa to leave.

Ten minutes later, Alexa's car pulled into her driveway. By now she was in tears. Mrs. Sherman glanced out the back window.

She waited patiently in the kitchen for Alexa. After a few minutes, she peeked her head out the side door and smiled. She followed her smile with a wave.

Alexa didn't answer. Instead, she continued to cry from the front seat of the car. Alexa's face and mouth contorted she was crying so hard.

Her mom's smile turned into a frown. She slowly walked towards the passenger side of Alexa's car.

Her mom slung the dishrag she was carrying over her shoulder as she opened the passenger car door. She sat in the bucket seat and looked at Alexa compassionately. Alexa did everything in her power not to look at her mom. She continued to cry.

Tears continued to run down Alexa's face. As hard as she tried to stop, she couldn't.

For several minutes, Alexa and her mom sat silently in the car. Mrs. Sherman ran her hand up and down Alexa's arm.

Finally, after several minutes, Alexa's tears subsided.

Alexa looked at her mom. Her mascara was smeared all over her face and her lips quivered.

"Mom?"

Silence.

"Why are people so mean?"

"Well sweetie...some people are jealous of others. Other people fear things that are new, and other people have been raised to think or act a certain way. It's not always their fault."

"I love those two girls. They're great friends, but sometimes they're not so great. They were mean to me today."

"What about?"

"Oh, because I went out with Julio Friday night."

Alexa's head rested against the back of her seat. The right side of her face was covered by her blonde hair.

"Sweetie," her mom said as she ran her left hand through her daughter's hair, "YOU have to determine ultimately what's the most important to you and go with it.

Can you date Julio and no longer be friends with Nicole and Janet, or is their friendship the most important? This is something only YOU can decide."

Her mom paused momentarily.

"Sweetie, if I know you, you can handle both. I have seen you grow up. You are genuine, mature, and a good natured young lady. I have seen those two girls rely on you. You're the straw that stirs their drink. They can be difficult BUT they can be good friends and have been good friends to you since you moved here."

She paused. "As long as Julio treats you well and makes you happy AND you make him happy, your friendship should continue."

Alexa looked at her mom with fresh tears in her eyes. "Thanks mom, I love you."

"I love you too sweetie, just hang in there. Nothing worth having is easy."

Mrs. Sherman patted Alexa softly on the leg. "Sit in here as long as you need to. Just know your dad and I are here for you."

Her mom got out of the car and made her way back into the house.

A sad smile worked across Alexa's face after several

minutes of thought.

13

Late December

Mike Williams

Sadly, Christmas break was near at its end. Much to Julio's surprise, the temperatures remained in the 40's for the whole two weeks. Quite a change from northern Illinois.

As he laid on his bed the last Friday of break, baseball and Alexa were the two main constants which popped into his head. They talked on the phone and texted some over break, but the conversation of another date had not yet come up.

He scrolled to her number and just looked at it for several minutes while he debated with himself.

Up to this point, Alexa had taken the initiative to call Julio. He knew he had to take some initiative at some point.

After some contemplation, he dialed her number.

On the other end he could hear her phone ring. *Crap! There's no going back now* he thought.

After two rings, Alexa picked up the phone.

"Hello?" she thought gleefully to herself.

"Hey Alexa. It's Julio," he replied shyly.

She giggled. "I know that you big goof, how are you?"

His voice shook. "Um, I didn't know if you wanted to get some hot cocoa in Carbondale this afternoon."

Alexa lit up like a firefly in the night. She ran from one end of her room to the other, frantically excited.

Though excited, she thought she would have some fun with him. "Oh I don't know, it's a little short notice, don't you think?"

He felt defeated already. "I...I just was lying here and thinking I haven't seen you in a few days so I thought I would ask."

Alexa, ever the humanitarian, could tell he was in pain. "I'm teasing you...you big lunk! I'd love to get some hot cocoa with you. What time are you thinking? I can be ready in thirty minutes?"

"Did you just call me a big lunk?"

"What are you going to do about it?" Alexa asked playfully.

"I'll be over there in thirty minutes."

Alexa hung up her phone.

"Mom, I'm going with Julio to Carbondale for some cocoa!"

Julio opened the door to his room and yelled down the stairs to his mom. "Hey mom, Alexa and I are going to

Carbondale for a bit."

Both moms smiled in their respective houses, even if it was short notice.

Julio threw on a pair of pants, a t-shirt, and a blue sweater. He galloped down the stairs.

"Well look at you all cheery!" his mom said with a smile.

His cologne drifted ever so softly towards his mom. "And you're wearing cologne. Wow! You smell good." She paused. "When was the last time you wore cologne?"

"Mom..." he followed up embarrassingly.

He couldn't get out of the house fast enough.

"We're going to Carbondale for a hot cocoa. Bye!"

Before she could respond Julio was out the door.

Back at the Sherman household, Alexa was happily humming to herself like a songbird in the summer. She threw on her favorite pair of dark jeans, a pair of brown boots with a black buckle, and her favorite red sweater. Lastly, once dressed, she spritzed herself with perfume.

As soon as she sprayed herself with the perfume, she heard a car pull in the driveway. In a panic she ran to the window because she heard country music booming from the car radio.

"Julio doesn't listen to country," she muttered to

herself.

"What the..." she said to herself as Julio got out of the car.

Julio walked up to the door, still slightly afraid of her parents. As he was about to knock, the door swung open.

"Hey Mrs. Sherman, how are you today?"

"So, where are you guys going?" she asked sternly.

Julio nervously stood on the porch.

Mrs. Sherman smiled. "I'm just giving you a hard time. She should be ready shortly, why don't you come on in."

Before Julio had a chance to move towards the door, Alexa passed her mom and grabbed his arm.

"Sorry Julio, my mom can be a meanie sometimes. C'mon, let's get out of here."

"Well you two kids have a good time. I see Alexa is in a big toot to get you out of here, Julio!" Mrs. Sherman yelled as Alexa lead him away.

Mrs. Sherman watched them as they walked towards the car. Finally, she closed the door to the house and went inside. She couldn't help but watch her daughter and Julio from behind the curtain.

Much to Alexa's surprise, Julio walked around to her side and opened up her car door. She wasn't used to that.

Sadly, most of us at Franklin High School weren't as smooth as Julio.

As he walked around to the driver's side, Alexa watched him intently. She couldn't take her eyes off him.

"We need to take your car sometime." He said with a smile.

Alexa laughed. "Why's that? You already tired of driving me around?"

"No...I just want to see what this beautiful blonde next to me is like when she drives."

Alexa flipped her wavy hair to her side and smiled gleefully at Julio. "Okay then. Get your butt out! We're going to take my car."

"Are yah sure? You don't mind driving? I wasn't trying to get out of driving."

"Shut up you big dork. I'm driving. Besides, I love driving my car."

He smiled. "Again. You called me a dork. I'm not a fan of this name calling."

Alexa laughed. She clicked the car remote which unlocked the doors. He immediately noticed the leather interior.

"You ready?" she said with a laugh.

As soon as the engine came on, country music blared from the radio.

She poked him playfully in the side. "Here's your music. I hear you're a country fan."

Alexa turned the radio volume up and down as she drove. It all depended on the song. Needless to say, by the time they reached the coffee place just outside of Carbondale, not much was said between the two.

As they walked up to the coffee place, Julio admired Alexa's walk. She had a certain sway he admired and loved.

He looked at Alexa. "You look amazing."

She smiled. "Thanks! So do you."

As they waited to order, she leaned up against him. She put her arm around him and kissed his arm. He looked down and smiled.

He couldn't help but smell her hair. It had fruity smell to it. They stood quietly in line. Alexa looked up and smiled.

He quickly realized the complexities of even the simplest things, like placing an order for hot cocoa. He could tell Alexa was a pro. Julio belonged in the minor leagues. She seemed to know the ins and outs, low fats and creams, while Julio thought a hot chocolate was a hot chocolate. As long as it had whipped cream on top with sprinkles as a bonus, he was good. He didn't know this endeavor would be so complex.

They finally finished their drinks. Alexa looked at Julio and smiled flirtingly. "So how was your hot chocolate?"

"It was good."

She smiled. "Good. Glad you thought so. That hit the spot. Thanks for asking me. You ready to go?"

He smiled at her. "Yeah, let's get out of here."

She hopped down from her chair and poked Julio in the side.

They both were quiet as they made their way home. If for no other reason, they were both happy.

"So... are you ready for baseball?"

He grinned. "Seriously? You have to ask that?"

"Hey! Just call me a Nosie Nelly," she said with a smile.

"Yeah! I can't wait, though I'm a bit nervous."

Alexa squeezed his hand, confirming her support.

They gradually approached Franklin. The winter air had set in once the sun crept below the horizon.

"Alexa, I wanna thank you for your company."

"No no. I wanna thank you. I feel very comfortable around you."

They turned onto Alexa's street. She pulled the car into

the driveway and stopped.

Julio looked at Alexa. "I hope we can do this again."

Fighting tears, she grinned and nodded. "You make me feel like I can be myself. I hope we do this sooner than later. And Julio, there will be times my friends will be mean. I'm sorry for them being jerks."

"No worries. I'll see you on Monday."

He leaned over and gave Alexa a hug. Once out of the car, Alexa walked Julio to his car. They stood at the car door. A momentary silence filled the air. Finally, Alexa threw both arms around him. Julio squeezed back enthusiastically.

After a minute's embrace, he regrettably let her go. Julio jumped in his car and slowly backed out of the driveway. Alexa moved to the top of the porch and turned back towards the street. With her hand she blew him a kiss. Julio smiled. In return, he flashed his lights. Ecstatic her antics were seen, she turned, flipped her hair off her shoulders, and walked into the house happily grinning.

14

Early March

Mike Williams

The winter came and went. Throughout the winter months of January and February, Alexa and Julio would go for a hot chocolate or pizza. Most times they drove to Carbondale, because it was the simplest place to go. Let's face it. Franklin didn't have a whole lot to do. And to be honest, Julio didn't know any better places in the area either.

As March slowly approached, Julio prepared himself for another baseball season. He was excited to play for Coach Wilson and even more excited to prove us wrong. I couldn't wait for the season to start as well.

The morning of tryouts, Julio's alarm went off. It was the loudest buzz you could have imagined. His eyes slowly opened. He rolled over and put the alarm on snooze.

Before he jumped out of bed, he stretched one more time. He looked across the room and noticed Jeremy was still asleep. Quietly, he walked over to Jeremy's bed, grabbed him by the shoulders and shook him lightly. "Hey, wake up, wake up!"

Jeremy quickly opened his eyes. "No, I don't wanna get up," he muttered.

The two moved throughout the room like a couple of zombies. Even Julio, who was ten times more excited than his brother, moved in slow motion. After Julio put on his jeans and t-shirt, he looked at his baseball bag.

Even though he went through his bag the night before, he wanted to make doubly sure he had everything. He never understood those players who showed up unprepared. Needless to say, that irritated the heck out of me as well.

Gleefully, he turned and looked at his brother. "It's time to go to school, Jer."

Jeremy rubbed his eyes. He was still aggravated about his early wake up.

"This is our time, Jeremy. Let's embrace it."

While they prepared for the day upstairs, their mom was in the kitchen frantically preparing them breakfast. A tradition since Julio's freshmen year. Sadly, I didn't have that tradition. Those lucky jerks.

Like a thundering herd of horses, Julio and Jeremy came down the stairs and into the kitchen.

"Mom, Mom, hey Mom," they yelled simultaneously.

She smiled. Before she even had a chance to answer them, they were in the kitchen. "Well, good morn boys." She said quietly. "I have made you some pancakes and bacon."

Julio's and Jeremy's eyes expanded like saucers when they saw the spread of goodies on the kitchen table their mom had fixed for them.

Before their mom could even tell them to grab a plate, Julio had put some pancakes and bacon on his plate. Mrs. James did her best to move out of their way.

She leaned up against the counter in her robe and held a cup of coffee. "So, are you guys excited about today?"

Julio looked at his mom and smiled. Jeremy was still a bit overwhelmed.

"Mom, I'm looking forward to this afternoon. I have to admit I'm slightly nervous though," Julio said surprisingly.

"Julio, you're going to wow them. I am so proud of you. You have handled this year with dignity. I'm so thankful everyday you are my son!" She looked in Jeremy's direction. "Jeremy."

"Yeah mom?" he replied curiously.

"Be yourself. Don't try to be your brother. You have ability too," she said with a smile.

"Ability!" Julio exclaimed looking at Jeremy. "Bro, I am telling you right now, you can be better than me."

Jeremy didn't respond though his facial expression said it all. He didn't believe his brother.

Julio looked at his mom as he shoved the last few bites from his plate into his mouth. "Thanks for the breakfast. Excuse me, I need to get ready." Julio pulled out his chair, took his plate to the sink, and ran upstairs leaving Jeremy downstairs by himself alone at the table.

Jeremy looked around surprised by the sudden disappearance of his brother. His mom was still leaning against the counter though she was now on her second cup of coffee. She smiled at Jeremy.

In a moment of honesty Jeremy looked up at his mom. "I'm scared. I wish I had the confidence he has. Every day I'm scared," he said looking down at his plate.

Saddened, Mrs. James looked at her youngest son. "You'll be fine. Just do your best. Have I mentioned I'm proud of you too?"

"Thanks mom, I appreciate it." He stood up and stretched. "Well...I guess I better get goin. Otherwise Julio will leave me here."

He gathered his plate and silverware and looked at his

mom. "Thanks for the breakfast mom, you're the bomb!" Before she could respond he was upstairs preparing for school.

The day slowly passed. We sat in Foods class, our last class of the day. The clock seemed to move in slow motion. Our teacher, Ms. Seymore, seemed to be talking endlessly about fruits or something. I know I wasn't paying attention and I'm sure Julio wasn't either. All that mattered was baseball.

He glanced up at the clock and noticed a minute remained in the period. Julio looked around the room. Alexa caught his eye. She was sitting in a desk on the opposite side of the room. She smiled, looked at the clock, and then at Julio. She winked and tapped her heart two times with her middle and index fingers. She followed that with a tap to her lips two times with the same fingers.

Julio smiled. As if it was a secret handshake Julio copied Alexa moving his fingers to his heart and then to his lips.

As soon as he tapped his fingers to his lips the bell rang. We sprang to our feet. If you didn't know any better you would've thought we were trying to escape from a firing squad. As we hurried out the door Ms. Seymore could be heard rambling on about something related to class. Hey the bell had rung, she had missed her chance.

Finally, Julio made it to the locker room. He must have gotten held up in the Franklin hallway traffic because I beat him by a couple of minutes. He walked into the locker room and sat down on one of the benches that ran the length of the locker room. Several of us were already in the dressing room changing.

"Hey boy, are you ready to make a fool of yourself," muttered Ronald.

Julio looked up, stared at him for a moment, and then went back to changing into his baseball cloths.

"Did you hear me boy! I'm talking to you," Ronald blasted. Of all the people Ronald was the last one who should have been talking trash. Even though Ronald was a two year starter and junior he was an idiot at times and an average player at best.

Julio looked at Ronald first then the rest of us. He looked back at Ronald. "Boy? I will strike your loud butt out when given the chance. Do you ever shut up? Damn." Julio stood up, smiled, and walked out of the locker room.

We immediately started to make fun of Ronald since Julio got the best of him. Ronald sat on the bench in disbelief.

"He got you," I said as I pointed my finger at ole Ronald. One of the guys, can't remember who, fell off the bench because he was laughing so hard.

Ronald looked at me angrily. "Shut up."

John, one of the seniors, chimed in. "I cannot wait to see him strike your butt out, you know it will happen! Heck you can't even hit your way out of a paper sack!"

Julio made his way into the gym after he left us in the locker room. He immediately counted the number of those trying out for the team. To his surprise there were only twenty in the gym including the ones in the locker room. What a contrast to West Aurora which usually consisted of seventeen trying out from just one class.

Most of us were dressed in sweatpants and a t-shirt sporting the Franklin school colors. Granted we were in a small town so everyone knew everyone but you could tell almost immediately who had never picked up a glove in their life. A couple of the guys looked rather awkward in their sweat pants and t-shirt. I actually felt sorry for them.

Coach Wilson barked for us to circle up. He immediately pointed to Zach and John to lead us as we stretched. I always wondered why all the coaches pointed to Zach as a leader. Granted he was talented but he wasn't always a great leader. Maybe they saw something in him I didn't at the time.

As we stretched Julio looked from side to side. He didn't even realize Jeremy was next to him. If it was any other time Jeremy would have stayed clear of his brother, but since this was our first practice and we had been less than welcoming I could understand why. I think Julio was actually glad his brother was there by his side.

While Julio stretched he watched Coach Wilson walk around the circle. On the other side of the group was his assistant coach, Don Jacobs.

Don was a good sized man. He was 6'5" tall with short blonde hair and he looked as if he could put a hurt on the baseball. He apparently pitched for St. Louis for several years. Needless to say we thought that was awesome especially since we lived in "Cardinals Country."

After stretching for five to ten minutes, Zach looked at Coach. "We're done sir."

"What are you all waiting for then. Get loosened up!"

The twenty of us all pointed to each other as if our life depended on this choosing. We all tried to pick a friend to loosen up with. Julio looked at Jeremy and motioned for him to get a baseball. Enthusiastically, Jeremy ran to the bucket of balls. Coach stopped him by the arm.

Jeremy was caught off guard. He looked at Coach. "Sir?"

"I don't want you to throw with your brother, throw with someone else," Coach said sternly.

"Sir?" Jeremy replied again.

"What do you not understand about that? Throw with Ronald. Damn!" Coach looked at Ronald and pointed to him. Ronald slumped his shoulders. The last two people he wanted to throw with were Julio and Jeremy. It was kind of funny if you ask me.

Unenthused, Jeremy moved a few steps over so as to stand directly across from Ronald. He noticed Ronald had a ball so he dropped his.

Coach motioned to Zach. "Throw with Julio."

"Yes sir," he muttered. I was glad coach didn't single me out to throw with Julio. Not because he was black or anything like that, but in all honesty he threw way too hard for my liking.

The gym was quiet except for the popping of baseballs into gloves. Coach hated when ball players talked while loosening up. He stressed discipline and focus above all else once we walked onto ball the field until the moment we walked off. Of course there was always that freshmen that had to learn the hard way.

Julio and Zach wound up on the far end of the gym. Next to Julio was his brother. Though they were new they could tell talking wasn't allowed which was fine to them since this was their sanctuary.

Julio was glad he had been throwing all winter because his arm felt great. After a few minutes Julio noticed Zach's throws were coming at him harder. Julio was more than happy to pick up the speed as well. Before long, they were throwing the ball across the gym in a flat trajectory, often called a "rope."

Before long, the other guys glanced to their left or right depending on the side of the gym floor they stood. I know I had to peek over a few times as well. Many of the guys tried not to turn their head to much so as not to appear interested or impressed. Instead, they looked out of the corner of their eye.

Zach normally wore a batting glove when he threw to protect his hand, but Ronald didn't have a strong arm so Zach kept his batting glove in his baseball pants. Almost immediately Zach regretted not wearing his batting glove. He knew he couldn't pause to put it on out of pride or stubbornness. Take your pick.

Each time Zach received the ball from Julio he winced in pain. His fingers began to throb. Several times Zach muttered *ugh that hurt* to himself.

Coach Jacobs watched the duel between Zach and Julio. He smiled. At one point he glanced across the gym in the direction of Coach Wilson who was watching it play out as well. They both tried to hide their smiles, but weren't very successful.

Eventually, after throwing for ten minutes everyone on the team was loose. Coach Wilson looked at his watch and with a short grunt yelled "GO TO YOUR STATIONS!"

Coach Wilson's voice echoed throughout the gym. On key, everyone stopped throwing and put the baseballs we were using in the bucket, and quickly ran to the station we were assigned. Of course, a few of the freshman ran around like chickens with their heads cut off because they had no clue what the heck they were doing or where they were going. Again, they learned to refer to the practice schedule posted on the wall unless they wanted to get a butt chewing.

I stood at the batting cage and smiled. *Freshmen, I* thought.

Julio and his brother ran to the batting cages as well. It was their first station. The batting cage was set up in one corner of the gym. Most schools in southern Illinois were jealous of us. The batting cage consisted of a blue net with *Franklin* spelled out on the back end. The net extended sixty feet in length, eight feet high, and about seven feet wide with an L shaped screen net on one end for the players to throw behind. I have to say it was honestly pretty cool.

Zach, Ronald, John, Jeremy, Julio, and I were assigned to the same group. I was kind of surprised Jeremy was in our group since he was a freshmen but I wasn't the one who made the practice schedule. After one practice though I understood why he was grouped with us.

Coach Wilson walked over to the cage from the far end of the gym. He looked at Ronald, "I want you to throw first."

The gym was quiet except for Coach Wilson and Jacobs moving through the gym instructing, the clanging of bats hitting baseballs, and the sounds of balls rolling on the gym floor. None of us talked while awaiting our time to hit. We knew what was good for us. Of course Ronald's exchange with Julio prior to practice heightened the intensity. From my observations it seemed to bother us more than Julio.

Zach hit first. Each ball Zach hit was lined back at Ronald

better than the previous one. After the seventh ball, Zach stepped out from under the net and looked at Julio. "Show us what you got boy."

Julio stepped into the cage. He let the bat lazily swing like a pendulum as he wiped the few beads of sweat from his brow. Julio nodded to Ronald. Ronald tossed the first ball. Julio swung. Unimpressively the ball hit the bat and weakly fluttered behind Julio. Zach, John, and I all looked down. We did everything in our power not to laugh. I was the most successful of the three. I nudged Zach with my arm. He, of course, playfully nudged me back.

Julio stepped away from the rubber plate, gathered himself, and stepped back in. He again let the bat swing like a pendulum as he did previously...then came set. Ronald threw ball two.

SMACK, CLANK!

The ball hit the top part of the L screen so hard, the L screen fell onto Ronald. Zach and John looked at each other as if that was a fluke. He could not repeat it. Right? As for me, my mouth dropped open with amazement.

Ronald set the screen back up and threw pitch three. Again SMACK! The sound of the bat hitting the ball echoed throughout the gym. Zach, John, and I all looked at each other rather amazed.

After a strong round in the cage Julio worked his way out from underneath the net. He looked at Zach and smiled.

Zach looked at Julio and muttered "nice hitting."

I could tell Ronald was glad Julio stepped out of the cage. Probably glad for his own safety.

After several weeks of practice our first game was thankfully only a week away. I mean you can only practice for so long. Coach had the team meet in his room after school the Friday before our first game. It was the perfect day to hand out uniforms because it was rainy outside. We received two jerseys. One was solid white while the other one was solid blue. The number was the opposite color of the jersey top and the word *Franklin* was in script on the front. We also received two pairs of pants, one blue and one white. The solid blue was personally my favorite.

After he passed out the uniforms Coach had us sit in the hall outside his room. He called us in individually. It was always nerve racking but I appreciated it as well. Some of the guys came out of the room with smiles while others weren't so happy when they came out of the room.

Finally after calling in each player, even his brother, Julio was called into the room. Like the rest of us, Coach

Wilson had Julio sit in a student desk across from the two coaches. Each coach had a notebook with writing scrawled on it. Julio sat in the desk and nervously waited to hear from his coaches.

Coach Wilson looked at his assistant and then Julio. "So how do you like it here so far?"

Julio sat back and looked at each coach. "Well it's been rough, but I like my teachers and I look forward to playing for you guys."

"Is there anything I can do to make it better for you here?" Coach Wilson asked.

Julio sat up as he contemplated that question. "If you forced these guys to like me and accept me then I won't be accepted. My brother and I have to prove ourselves. If in turn we are never accepted, then it's not to be. I don't feel threatened anymore though."

Coach Jacobs looked at Coach Wilson and then Julio. "Do you feel we have your back?"

Julio looked at Coach Jacobs. "Yep."

Coach Wilson paused. "Well we wanted to let you know we're impressed with your pitching therefore you'll be our main pitcher. When you're not pitching you'll probably play right field. Do you have any questions for us?"

Julio smiled, "no sir."

"Okay then, we'll see you Monday."

15

Late March

Mike Williams

The sun rudely came through Jeremy's and Julio's bedroom window. Julio rolled over and hit the off button on his alarm. He laid in the bed and stretched. The alarm read 6:30 but to Julio it felt much earlier.

He rolled out of bed and sluggishly made his way into the bathroom.

"Get your butt up, Jer," he muttered as he passed his brother.

Jeremy grunted and rolled over.

After fifteen minutes, Julio came out of the bathroom fully awake from the warm shower. He looked at his brother who was still in bed. Julio's shoulders slumped. "Get your lazy butt up, man."

Jeremy rolled back over, looked at his brother, stretched for moment and began to reluctantly get out of bed.

"Bro, sometimes I worry about you," Jeremy muttered.

After belting out an evil laugh, Julio smacked his brother on the backside with his towel as he walked lazily to the shower.

Once Jeremy staggered into the bathroom, Julio began to get dressed. After he put on his blue sweats and t-shirt, he grabbed his newest Franklin hoodie. He lifted his bag up to his bed and ruffled through it to make sure he had everything needed for the day. Even though solid blue wasn't his favorite uniform he thought it had a cool look to it.

After going through the bag, Julio scanned the room to make sure he didn't leave any of his gear behind. He zipped up his bag and commenced walking out of the room. He paused. "I'm going downstairs."

There was no reply from inside the bathroom. Julio was surprised with Jeremy's less than excited demeanor after being told the day before he would be the starting catcher.

The clock read 7:00 as Julio ran down the stairs as if it was Christmas morning and he could not wait to see what Santa brought him.

Not long after arriving in the kitchen, his mother followed behind him. She walked into the kitchen and noticed Julio at the table by himself eating a bowl of cereal. "Did you find everything, sweetie?" she asked curiously.

"Yep," Julio responded as he shoved cereal into his

mouth.

"Did you sleep well last night?" she asked.

"Yep," he responded.

She looked at him with a smile. Julio looked back and smiled. "So tell me about this team you're playing today. Are they any good?" She asked as she fumbled for a glass for her juice.

Julio continued to shove his cereal into his mouth, but managed to respond to his mom in between bites. "I'm not really sure. From what I've gathered this is one of the weaker teams we'll be playing."

"Are you excited about starting this game on the mound?" she asked with a smile.

"Don't know if excited is the word mom, but I'm looking forward to it. I think it's kind of cool Jeremy will be catching me. I just hope he can handle my stuff," he added sarcastically. If anyone could catch him it was his little brother.

Eventually Jeremy staggered into the kitchen. He quietly ate his breakfast while Julio drank his midsize glass of orange juice. After some time had passed, Julio looked at the clock. The time was now 7:45 and Julio was ready to get the party started.

He looked at his little brother. "We want to head out around 8:30 at the latest. I want to hit in the cages before everyone else gets there."

Jeremy, who was still not awake yet, looked at his big brother. "Sounds good." He knew he had no choice in the matter.

Jeremy's stomach was in knots and he felt like he was going to vomit. He did his best to hide his nerves.

Julio and Jeremy were the first to arrive at the field. Coach Wilson drove up and noticed Julio's car. He smiled when he saw the two hitting in the cages. He still couldn't believe Julio was in the program. Not only was he a good player, but he showed dedication to the game and everything about it. Several times prior to practice, Julio would walk around the infield and gather up the small rocks that could create a bad hop. Sometimes Zach would assist, but they never walked together. Truth be told, as time went on, I did it was well. It was all because of Julio.

Coach Wilson drove up to the cages and rolled down his window. He leaned out of the window and yelled at Jeremy. "You been here long?"

Jeremy looked at his coach. "We've been here for about one hour or so. Not sure. What time is it?"

Coach Wilson laughed. "Well just don't wear yourselves out to much. We do have a game you know."

Jeremy nodded his head, hoping his brother had heard his coach as well.

Soon, other cars began to arrive. First Coach Jacobs, and then, soon after, the rest of the team. As the rest of us arrived, we worked our way over to the cages to hit. By this time Julio and Jeremy had their share of hitting and gladly conceded the cages.

An hour before the game, the bus for Jackson County arrived. The sun was high in the sky and there were absolutely no clouds. There was a slight breeze, but not enough to make a difference as long as you were dressed appropriately, which I thankfully was. As soon as the bus arrived, we began to change out of our practice clothes and into our uniforms.

While the rest of the team went out to right field to stretch, Jeremy and Julio remained in the dugout. Julio liked to loosen up thirty minutes prior to the game.

"Look at that boy sitting in there like he's so damn special," Zach said to Ronald quietly while they stretched.

Ronald looked into the dugout and then at Zach. "Yeah, I have a feeling he'll get rocked today. Shoot, he's nothing special."

Zach paused for a moment and then stood up from the ground, smacked his glove, and looked at Ronald. "Dude, what planet are you on? He's the best player out here, better than anyone on our team and definitely better than any of the players on Jackson's team that's for sure. I'm not happy about it, but it's true."

John looked at Ronald and then Zach. "You know Zach is right, don't you? I hate the fact a black guy is on our team but shoot, he sure is better than any of us out here. I will be surprised if anyone hits him today."

I listened in on the conversation and I totally agreed with Zach and John. I knew he was the best player on the team, for better or for worse.

Game time slowly approached. Parents and students alike arrived and sat on the bleachers. Some of the parents sat in lawn chairs near the bleachers. My parents always sat behind the bleachers for some reason. Thankfully they weren't loud or obnoxious.

Unlike mine, Julio's parents made it a habit not to sit next to the other parents. Instead, they sat well away from everyone. They each brought a lawn chair to sit in, like many of the other parents who did not sit in the bleachers.

Alexa arrived with Nicole. At one point Julio glanced over and noticed her in the stands. He looked at her and subtly waved.

After some time had passed, Alexa noticed Julio's parents. Without hesitation she stood up. Surprised, Nicole looked up at her. "Where are you going?"

Alexa looked at Nicole and then pointed beyond the dugout. "I'm goin over there, you wanna join me?" She asked with a smile.

"What?! You're going to go sit with those coons? I'd rather shoot myself," Nicole said sternly. A few others overheard the conversation which brought out a smattering of giggles and laughs.

"Well, I'd hate for your highness to lower yourself," Alexa replied forcibly.

Alexa stepped down from the bleachers and walked towards Julio's parents. While making the journey, she passed several people who made comments that I would prefer not to repeat. She did all she could to ignore them. She was glad to be wearing her shades because a tear formed in the corner of her left eye. It took every ounce of energy not to cry.

Feeling slightly broken and accomplished she finally

made it to Julio's parents.

Mrs. James stood up enthusiastically when she noticed Alexa.

"Can I sit with you guys?"

Mr. James smiled. "You sure can. You don't even need to ask."

Alexa moved around to where Mrs. James was sitting and sat in the grass with her legs crossed. Alexa soon forgot about the walk and a smile came across her face.

"We were hoping you'd be at the game," Mrs. James said with a smile. "Do you not have a blanket?"

"No ma'am, I don't," Alexa replied.

"Well here, sit on this one." Mrs. James pulled a blanket out of her bag. Alexa's mouth dropped. She couldn't get over the bag of goodies Julio's mom brought to the game. She looked at Alexa and laughed. "Sweetie, I have two boys, one seventeen and one fourteen. We have gone to baseball games since Julio was in first grade. You do the math."

They both laughed.

"Well, thanks for the blanket Mrs. James." Alexa said with a huge much needed smile.

Mrs. James looked at Alexa and smiled. The two sat and talked about school and Southern Illinois. Finally, Franklin

High School headed onto the field which was followed by cheers from the students and parents from the Franklin side.

Julio stood atop the mound and Alexa proudly watched with a big grin. She looked at his mom. "Wow, your son sure looks big out there, Mrs. James," she said with a giggle.

Mr. James looked at her and sarcastically smiled. "You should see our food bills!" They all laughed.

The first batter for Jackson County High School stepped up to the plate. Julio stood with both feet on the rubber and held his glove up to his face, just enough to cover his nose. The numbers on his back, 34, looked bigger than ever because of his size. He took a deep breath. Jeremy gave his brother a big target on the inside part of the plate. Julio moved into his wind up. He released the pitch and instantly both Jeremy and the batter could hear a "zzzzzzz" as the seams on the ball buzzed through the air towards home at ninety-five miles per hour. Surprised by the speed, the batter stood there frozen.

Strike one.

Julio's career at Franklin High School had begun.

16

Early May

Mike Williams

Even though we nearly lost to Carbondale in extra innings, we built a solid 12-0 record through the month of April. Somehow we were able to pull out a victory. Julio had quickly made a name for himself in Southern Illinois. In several games, the opponents got three hits or less. In the majority of games, he struck out at least ten batters. I mean, the dude was throwing gas. In many of the games I stood over at third base and admired what he was able to do. Like me, Julio had also become a home run threat.

Almost every day Coach Wilson's phone rang. College recruiters were now expressing interest in our newest Franklin resident. Most of the recruiters were from small colleges in Illinois, Missouri, and Kentucky though.

As the season went on, more and more people started to come to the games as well. A buzz of excitement developed throughout the school over our team and our success. The next biggest opponent was Vienna, possibly our biggest baseball rival in the area.

Coach Wilson finished his class early. Jake, the ever

talkative student and teammate, turned towards Julio. "So are we going to win this weekend?" he asked confidently.

Julio shrugged his shoulders. "I don't know, I've heard Vienna is good. Don't know how they compare to us though."

Jake smiled. "Well, you're pitching right?"

"Yeah," Julio replied shyly.

"Well then we'll win," Jake said confidently.

Even though Jake rarely played, he was just happy to be a part of the team. Not only did Julio admire Jake's attitude but I did as well.

Julio smiled. "Thanks for your confidence."

The bell rang. It was time for Julio to wander off to gym while I begrudgingly made my way to Spanish.

Julio walked by Coach who stopped him. "I want you to give this to Coach Smith. This is a pass for you to come back to my room. I need to talk to you."

A few minutes later, Julio appeared at Coach Wilson's door.

"Ahhh come on in Julio. Take a seat," coach said firmly.

Julio sat in one of the front seats, unsure why coach wanted to talk to him. Coach Wilson seemed preoccupied with straightening up his room so Julio waited patiently.

Coach Jones, the athletic director, soon appeared at the door with a smile.

He quietly knocked on the door.

Coach Wilson turned around. "Ahh -- come on in Coach."

Coach walked in and sat down next to Julio. He turned the desk so it would face Julio which made Julio unintentionally nervous. Did he do anything wrong? Dang, he didn't think he did but the coaches seemed to be overly serious. Coach Wilson picked up a pad of paper from his desk and rearranged one of the student desks so as to face Julio.

Coach Wilson cleared his throat. "Are you wanting to play college ball, and if so, where do you want to go?"

Julio looked at Coach Wilson and then Coach Jones.

Were they serious? Of course he wanted to play college ball!

"Yes sir, I do want to but I really haven't thought about where much."

"What about professionally?" asked Coach Jones.

Julio leaned forward in his desk. Somehow he was able to eek out a smile. "Yeah, that has been a goal of mine for some time, sir."

"Well Julio, there have been some coaches in the area already talking about you, which I'm not surprised with, but apparently a few scouts have talked to your former coach from West Aurora. Needless to say, word about you has followed you down here. I just wanted to give you a heads up and let you know. I will keep you and your parents informed if any schools or professional teams contact us."

"Okay, I appreciate it," Julio replied, thankful he wasn't in trouble.

Julio moved towards the door and paused. He looked back towards Coach Wilson and smiled. "Hey Coach, no worries about tomorrow. We got Vienna."

He approached the gym doors. Alexa happened to be in the hall. "Hey you big goof, shouldn't you be in class?" She walked towards him with the biggest smile. "Are we still on tonight for pizza?"

Julio proudly smiled. "Sounds like a plan. I'll see you round 6:30? I can't stay out late tonight because of tomorrow's game though."

Alexa giggled. "Ohhh I know, you're such a big stud athlete." She playfully puffed herself up to look bigger than she was. Alexa winked and continued on to her class, poking him in ribs as she walked by. He smiled and walked into the gym.

Julio and Jeremy drove up to the house after practice. Julio threw his gear and hat down on to the floor and sprinted upstairs to his room. As he ran into his room, he passed his mom who attempted to ask about his day, but he subtly told her he was in a hurry.

"Sure, sure, blow off your lowly ole mom for some young blonde, I see how it is."

Within minutes he was in the shower and washing off the practice grime. Julio jumped out of the shower and threw on a pair of jeans and a collared shirt. He stopped at his bedroom door and snapped his fingers. "I nearly forgot," he said out loud to himself. He nearly forgot to spritz himself with her favorite cologne.

As he made his way to the back door his dad walked in. "Whoa there son, what's the hurry? Did you have a good day?"

Julio stopped in front of his dad and mom, who happened to be greeting each other in the doorway.

"Hey guys," he said while panting. "Alexa and I are going to Carbondale for pizza. We won't be late cause of the game tomorrow."

"That's fine son, have a good time and be safe," Mr.

James said in his deep voice. He had the kind of voice any male actor would be impressed with. I know when I heard it for the first time I was in awe. "Was your day good?" he continued.

"The day was fine," Julio replied. "Oh, no biggie, but coach called me into his room to let me know some college coaches are expressing an interest in me."

Mr. James nearly spit up the water he was drinking. "Wait, what? No big day? You did just say colleges are expressing an interest in you?"

"Yeah I'll tell you more later, okay?"

"Okay but that's exciting news. Say hello to Alexa for us and tell her we'll be at the game tomorrow."

That was the signal for Julio to go. "No worries, I'll say hello to her, BUT, I won't tell her you'll be at the game tomorrow," he said embarrassingly. As he bounded down the steps and quickly walked away he waved goodbye to his parents.

Julio pulled into Alexa's driveway and walked up the sidewalk towards her house. Before he reached the bottom steps to the front porch the door swung open. "Well look who's here! I don't know if you have my permission tonight young man."

Alexa's dad stood on the porch with his hands on his side and smiled, though he tried hard not to. "I don't need to get my shotgun out do I? You know I like to hunt."

Alexa busted through the door and pushed her dad playfully out of the way. "Dad, will you shut up? It's bad enough he has to hear crap at school -- I got my dad trying to be funny."

Julio reached forward to shake her dad's hand but was pulled away by Alexa. "Dad, don't wait up," she said gleefully.

They made their way up towards Carbondale. Julio couldn't take his eyes off of her because she looked awesome in her jean skirt and cowboy boots. He reached across and gently grabbed her hand. She gently squeezed his hand in return.

Yep Alexa was the girl for him.

Julio and Alexa laughed and enjoyed each other's company the whole evening. Time always went by fast when they were together. He especially loved listening to her stories about California from when she was a little girl.

Near the end of dinner Alexa looked at him and smiled. "So..." she said in her fun flirty voice. "Are you ready for the game tomorrow?"

She looked at him with her big blue eyes and her big beautiful smile. She leaned forward and rested her elbows on the edge of the table. Her hair gently touched the table. Julio was mesmerized.

He shrugged his shoulders. "We're ready as we'll ever be." He paused. "I'm excited to go against them that's for sure."

Alexa smiled. "Well, you guys will be fine and I know you're going to pitch an awesome game."

There was a momentary silence as she reached across and squeezed his hands. She winked. "Dude, let's ditch this place, you have a game tomorrow."

Morning quickly came. It was game day! Julio and Jeremy woke up early because they were both excited about the game. Both of the teams were undefeated. We were also battling for the top spot in the region which would mean a bye and home field advantage all the way through the region tournament.

The game went pretty much as planned. Through five innings, Vienna wasn't able to score any runs nor hit the ball off of Julio. We were equally inept at scoring runs. I couldn't seem to hit my way out of a paper sack and Julio was just as bad. Zach and Jeremy were the only ones who had decent hits.

After shutting out Vienna through five, Julio made his way towards the dugout. Coach Wilson stopped him several feet from the dugout. Julio's head was down and he must have been deep in thought because he seemed to be caught by surprise. He looked at coach. Coach had a look in his eye Julio hadn't seen before. To be honest I hadn't seen that look either and I had played at Franklin High School since my freshman year.

Julio looked at Coach. "Don't worry sir, I got this. I'm feeling it." Before Coach Wilson was able to respond Julio was in the dugout. Coach, who was reassured by his pitcher's confidence, walked quietly to third base.

The sixth inning came and went. Neither us nor Vienna were able to score any runs, much less get anyone on base. The words we muttered when we returned to the dugout after making an out would surely have made you guys blush. We were so frustrated.

Walt Smith was Vienna's starting pitcher. He was a tall gangly lefty. At first glance he was nothing impressive. Well I, and the rest of the team, was quite wrong. That dude could flat out pitch, which explains why colleges were looking at him.

Much to our surprise, Walt made his way to the mound to start the seventh inning. I guess we were surprised because it was late in the game, but then again, he went through our lineup several times like a hot knife through butter. The first batter of the inning was good ole Ronald, who of course struck out weakly on three pitches. Why coach didn't have someone hit for him I'll never know. I mean, he didn't even come close to making contact.

The next batter was our centerfield Eric Kaufman. Eric was having one of those special years. He had thrown several runners out from centerfield over the course of the year, and he had a number of clutch hits as well. He fouled two down the third base line. With two strikes on him, he tried to gather his thoughts by stepping out of the batter's box. He glanced towards Coach at third. Eventually, he worked the count to three balls and two strikes.

Walt took a step off the mound. After taking a breath he stepped back up on to the mound. We yelled from our dugout as loud as we could in hopes of making a difference. Eric moved into his batting stance.

Walt stepped into his pitching motion. He exploded towards home! In a matter of seconds the ball was over the fence in left field. Eric threw his right arm into the air while clenching his fist. Our dugout exploded into one gigantic cheer. Eric sprinted the bases energized by his tie breaking hit.

He reached home and pointed directly at Julio. "This is your game now, bring it home."

Julio just tipped his helmet and smiled. What a cool cucumber.

After Eric's home run, Julio stepped to the plate. After a solid at bat, he flew out deep to centerfield. The inning was over. I and the rest of the defense sprinted onto the field. All we had to do was hold Vienna. Julio slowly and confidently walked towards the mound.

Behind home plate the Franklin High School fans cheered and yelled their support. It was pretty cool to hear actually. The first two batters came up to the plate and were out equally as fast. They both hit weak grounders to Zach at shortstop. After each play Julio pointed to Zach and smiled. In return Zach tipped his hat.

After outs one and two, our fans got louder and louder. Victory over Vienna crept closer and closer. The feeling made me shiver. One out remained before we were the clear number one team in the region. To add insult to injury for Vienna, Julio was throwing a no hitter.

Jeremy called time out and jogged out to the mound. He was slowly becoming a leader behind home plate. After looking around the infield, he looked back towards the batter. The sun forced Jeremy to squint.

"Bro, he's been behind you all day. Let's go after this guy and if we throw curves they cannot be for strikes."

Julio wiped his brow with his sleeve and nodded. Jeremy turned and jogged back to home plate.

Locked in, Julio struck the batter out on three fastballs. The final pitch amazed many of the scouts who were there. They could not believe it but Julio was clocked at 95, 98, and finally 100 miles per hour on the final pitch. I was just glad he was on our team and not Vienna's.

When the final pitch crossed home plate and into Jeremy's glove, our fans jumped up and down enthusiastically. Alexa threw her fists into the air and joyfully hugged Julio's mom.

We were now the top team in the region.

17

Early May

Mike Williams

The Monday after the game with Vienna was a fun day at school. Many of us couldn't stop talking about the win. Up to that point, the game against Vienna was the biggest one of the year. Heck, Julio and Zach were even on the front sports page of **The Southern Illinois Gazette**, the biggest newspaper in southern Illinois.

I walked into my first period class and to my surprise **Way to go Wildcats**, was written in blue. Yeah, I thought it was cool. Julio seemed a little embarrassed.

"Yeah, it was just a game," I overheard him saying. Just a game!? "Hell no, it was Vienna!"

Thankfully, the day went by rather fast. I was ready to get back out to the ballfield. The day couldn't have been nicer to practice. We were circled up to stretch when Coach Wilson walked to the center of the circle.

"Guys, we have a chance to do something special. You can't take your foot off the gas. Yes, we have Cartersville Saturday but we can't look past Jones's County or Granderson. It's one game at a time guys. We have four games left. Let's end strong."

After his quick speech he walked out of the circle and up to Coach Jacobs. "Do you think they know Cartersville is behind both Vienna and us?"

Coach Jacobs grinned. "It won't matter after we take care of business, coach."

"Yep I agree which is why today we're going to have an easy practice."

"Sounds good," Coach Jacobs said with a smile.

During practice, Zach walked up to Julio. "Hey Julio, great game the other day." He was grinning at Julio.

Caught off guard, Julio shyly smiled back. "Hey thanks. You had a good game too."

"Shoot man, I didn't do jack, but thanks anyways."

After an hour and half, Coach Wilson called us down to the right field line. We kneeled in the grass in rows two to three deep. He looked silently at Coach Jacobs and then us for several seconds.

"Guys, I'm proud of you for last Saturday's win -- but I'm telling you right now, if you forget about the task at hand, we will lose this week. We shouldn't lose, but that doesn't mean we won't. You guys are too good to let this season slip away. Just four more games." He held up four fingers. "I'm not going to waste anymore of your time talking, you know how I feel. Close out."

Wednesday's game was thankfully at home. Nothing was worse than a long bus ride on a weeknight in Southern Illinois. It certainly didn't hurt that the weather was absolutely perfect for baseball.

It was minutes before the game when Coach called for Julio.

"How's your arm feeling today? I ask because I have you in right today and you will be throwing Saturday. Are you good?"

Julio smiled confidently. "Coach, what do you mean am I good? I'm ready to whip some butt."

"Alright, that's all I needed to hear. Let's do it."

Julio grinned. "Sounds like a plan coach."

As it turned out, the biggest concern for us was whether to start Julio in right because we won convincingly. The team we were playing was greatly outmanned.

After the game, we raked and cleaned the field, something I hated to do but it had to be done. Once we finished, the team met in our usual spot in right field. Each player took a knee and waited attentively for Coach as he approached from the dugout. He walked up, looked at us, and held up three fingers.

He turned and walked away. "Close out guys."

We remained on our knees for several seconds unsure what to do. Coach had never had such a brief post-game talk before. We looked at each, rather confused.

Finally Zach jumped up. "Guys, let's get out of here. Great game tonight! We have three games left guys until regionals. We got this."

The coaches stood at the end of the dugout as we gathered our gear. "You know Don, this is the first time I've seen them all play and close out together like they mean it. I think we have a team."

Outside the dugout stood an older man. "Coaches, you'll be fine," the older man said with a laugh.

Surprised, Coach Wilson turned and stepped out of the dugout towards the voice. "Well look at this, Don. It's Jack Winters! What the hell are you doing here?!"

Jack Winters was a scout for St. Louis and a pretty respected one at that. The old geezer must have been in his 70s. Heck, the guy joined the Cardinals organization back in the 60s. He stood no taller than 5'5" and had a wiry built.

"You have someone on your team we may want."

"Well I'm here to help. Who is it you're interested in?"

"C'mon coach, you know who I'm referring to. When is that Julio kid pitching again?"

"Well, he will be pitching Saturday against Cartersville." A few of the players were still in the dugout so Coach did everything he could to keep his a voice down. No small challenge I must add.

"Cartersville, huh? Well, I just may have to see that game. You have a fun team to watch. This may be the best team to come out of Franklin in a long time."

"Well, thanks. Let's hope we can continue to play good ball."

"Oh I'm sure you will. Well... I'm going to head out. Good luck on Saturday."

The next two days flew by. We were more than ready to take on Granderson. In some ways, I actually felt bad for them.

Our starting pitcher was Kyle Whitten, a tall freshman. A team like Granderson was more his speed as opposed to Vienna or Cartersville.

Kyle made quick work of the Granderson batters. Their pitchers were no match for our offense. Home runs were hit by Julio, Zach, and Jeremy. Of course, Zach made it a point to tease me since Jeremy hit a homerun while I didn't.

Never mind I got several hits and his homer squeaked over the fence.

Like the night before, the team kneeled in right as we waited for Coach. He approached us with a faint smile. I mean, we did score 12 runs in five innings. He took his ball cap off and looked towards the regional signs in right field.

Silently he held up two fingers. It was time to take on Cartersville, a whole different beast compared to Jones County and Granderson.

18

Early May

Mike Williams

We got off the bus and were immediately impressed with the Cartersville field. It had been two years since I last played in Cartersville, so a quick glance was all I needed. This field was something out of the movies. The backstop was about fifty feet from home plate. Immediately behind the backstop were the bleachers. The bleachers stood fifty feet high and were made of brick. Brick! The bleachers fell twenty feet on each end. Music blared from the sound system which was truly awesome.

Jeremy approached the dugout and began to nudge his brother. Julio looked at Jeremy.

"What?!" he asked.

"Look out there. Damn," Jeremy whispered.

"Holy crap, it's the Green Monster," Julio stammered. He was referring to the giant green wall at Boston's Fenway Park.

Several of the guys had similar reactions to Julio's and Jeremy's. The left field fence was fifty feet high. The mammoth fence had all of the regional, sectional, and state titles nailed to the wall as well.

We quickly put our baseball shoes on and prepared to loosen up. Jeremy and Julio quietly sat on the bench and unpacked their equipment while the rest of us stretched in right field.

Julio leaned back on the bench. "Damn, what a beautiful field" he muttered to himself.

After a few minutes, he tapped Jeremy's leg with his glove. "Let's get loosened up."

"You nervous?" Jeremy asked.

"Nah man, just excited. Are you?"

Jeremy did not answer.

Together, they walked down the right field line towards the corner of the field. Zach noticed Julio and Jeremy as they passed him.

"Rock their world today, bud," Zach said with a devilish grin. Julio looked at Zach and nodded his head.

The brothers approached the corner of field. They threw down their gloves to stretch.

"Jeremy, do you see what I see? There are freaken speakers here!"

Jeremy didn't know what to make of this discovery. He was already a little nervous. For whatever reason the speakers made him even more nervous.

Jeremy noticed his brother's warmup pitches were slightly harder than normal. He knew his brother was amped. All he could think about was the pounding his hand was going to get. Imagine catching a ninety-five mile per hour fastball for at least five innings if not more. Yeah, Jeremy was a better man than me.

Julio's pregame ritual came to an end with a fastball down the middle. Jeremy held the pitch for a moment and smiled.

By now Cartersville had taken their pregame infield and outfield. We could tell Cartersville was for real. All of their throws were crisp and on target. Their infielders moved with confidence and swagger. *Not even Vienna carried themselves like this team* I thought.

Coach Wilson walked up to Julio. "Hey bud, remember, keep the ball away from their fourth hitter. I think he's going to Florida State to play. He's got some power. Otherwise, just go at these guys."

Julio hesitated. Once he realized Coach was done talking, he nodded and walked away.

"Please rise for the National Anthem," the voice from speaker blared.

Simultaneously, the fans stood up. We lined up along the first base foul line and the players from Cartersville stood along the third base foul line.

We pretended to look towards the flag in Centerfield which was conveniently over a sign which stated, **WELCOME TO CARTERSVILLE WHERE DREAMS END**.

Beyond the outfield fence was a hill. Julio hadn't noticed the hill until we were lined up on the foul line. On top of the hill were a series of pickups and grills. Fans had their own grills!

When the National Anthem came to the end, the Cartersville fans erupted. The noise seemed especially loud because of the brick bleachers.

Alexa and her friends, Nicole and Janet, stood up as well. They looked around in shock because the bleachers were shaking from the noise. It may have been the most vibrant crowd I had ever seen, not to mention the size of the crowd was fairly large.

The supporters for each team were easy to spot. Many of the Franklin High School fans wore dark blue while the Cartersville Tigers fans wore burnt orange.

The pitcher for Cartersville was Milt Smith. He was a tall, right handed senior with a nasty fastball and a wicked curve. After high school he apparently planned to play college baseball at one of the local junior colleges. Needless to say, we knew we had our hands full.

Zach, the lead-off hitter and the first batter of the game, stepped up to the plate to hit. He dug his cleats into the dirt around home like a dog burying its bone. He came set. Milt went into his motion. The first pitch whizzed down the middle of the plate for strike one. The Cartersville fans roared with excitement. The game had begun. Within three pitches, Zach was out. The next two batters didn't fare any better.

Our defense ran onto the field while Julio walked towards the mound. Cartersville not only had a great pitching staff, but their team was big and they hit the ball hard. They were bigger than us, that's for sure.

The first batter, who was one the quickest in the area, stepped into the batter's box. Julio and the batter worked the count to two balls and two strikes. Jeremy gave his brother the pitch selection -- a fastball low and away. Julio nodded in agreement. Julio stepped into his motion and stepped towards home plate. The pitch buzzed past the batter on the outer part of the plate exactly where Jeremy had set up.

"STRIKE THREE!" The umpire yelled.

In disbelief, the batter stood motionless at home. He backed out of the box, turned around and walked towards the dugout.

Like our batters, Julio worked through the first three Cartersville batters with ease. Two struck out while the third batter lazily flew out to left.

The next three innings were as eventful as the first inning. Neither team could hit the ball. Jeremy got into the act by throwing out one runner at second as he attempted to steal. Otherwise, both teams had very few on base.

As we jogged off the field at the end of the fourth inning, Coach Wilson stood outside the dugout and cheered us on.

"C'mon guys! Stand up and cheer your team on!" he yelled as he looked at the bench. In the background, music blared from the speakers. Even though there were three innings left, one could feel it may come down to one at bat, one mistake, or one stroke. I just hoped it was them making the mistake.

I stepped up to the plate to lead off the next inning. Throughout the year Coach had I and Julio alternate between the three and four spots in the lineup. For whatever reason Coach had me hitting fourth against Cartersville. All day Milt threw the ball in the mid-nineties. He showed no signs of letting up. The first pitch of the inning was thrown to home plate. The ball had no movement and it was down the middle of the plate, so I greeted it with a loud clank. As soon as the ball was hit, it was obvious. That's right! I hit a homerun.

I rounded third with the dumbest smile on my face. I hit Coach's hand with enthusiasm and jogged towards home. When I reached home, I stopped, paused, and pounded home plate with both of my feet. Enjoying every second I pointed towards the bleachers where the Franklin High School fans stood. In response, they cheered. It was a great feeling.

It was like a fire ignited the rest of the team. The next batter up lined a double down the left field line. Following the double, Jeremy drove in the runner on second with a single to right. The inning came to a close after the next batter struck out and the eighth batter grounded into a double play. Our team was up by two though!

Our defense ran onto the field. This was our game now. We had our best pitcher on the mound and a lead. It was obvious though, the fans from Cartersville weren't going to allow their team to stop fighting. The first Cartersville batter received a standing ovation from the fans as he walked up to the plate to hit.

The first batter up was their fourth batter in the lineup. He was quite the foe I have to say. As the batter approached, Jeremy turned towards the umpire. "Timeout blue."

The umpire threw his hands in the air. "Time!"

Jeremy took off his mask and jogged towards the mound.

Our coaches looked at each other. "I wonder if they are going to go after this guy or stay away from him like we had talked about," Coach Wilson muttered, fearful for the worst.

Back on the field, Jeremy walked up to Julio. "Hey bro, let's be smart with him. We're up by two." His glove covered his mouth so no one could read his lips.

"Get your ugly ass behind home. Damn."

Jeremy hesitated. "He's good man, let's be smart."

Julio didn't reply. Jeremy turned and jogged back to home plate.

The first two pitches were fastballs for strikes on the outer part of the plate. Each time Jeremy moved a little farther out on the corner of the strike zone and Julio kept hitting the spot.

"I hope he throws an off speed pitch here," Coach Wilson muttered to Coach Jacobs.

Instead, Julio threw a fastball!

The pitch zinged home. The batter was fooled! On three straight fastballs the batter was called out on strikes. *Hot damn*, I thought over at third. That was a big out.

"Yeah, that a boy," Coach Wilson yelled with his hands in the air.

Julio pointed towards home plate and acknowledged his brother.

The next two batters struck out and grounded out to me at third respectively to end another scoreless inning. Julio walked towards the dugout.

I passed him in a sprint and hit him on his butt with my glove. "Keep it going!"

Julio nodded his head.

Awaiting Julio by the dugout was Coach Wilson. "How are you feeling? Can you go the next two innings?"

Julio walked by Coach Wilson but did not respond. Both coaches looked at each other.

"This game is mine, Coach!" Julio barked adamantly.

"Well I guess he wants this game, Coach?" Coach Wilson said with a grin.

In the bleachers behind the dugout, our fans showed their support by cheering as we ran off the field. Alexa yelled as loud as she could, as did Nicole.

Sadly, we were held scoreless the next few innings. Julio walked to the mound at the beginning of the seventh. The score was still only two to nothing.

In between innings, Coach Wilson walked over to the freshmen, Kory Wilson. "You need to get loosened up in case we need you."

The first batter in the inning grounded out to Zach. The next batter grounded out to me.

Just one more out and the game would be over.

I was so excited I really didn't want the ball hit to me.

The lead was two with the lead off hitter due up. The fans stood up in support of their respective teams. The fans in the outfield started to honk their horns. I couldn't distinguish if they were for Franklin or Cartersville, but the sounds added a new dimension to the game. It was pretty cool.

After the second out, I tossed Julio the ball and smiled. "Go get' em." I added confidently.

Zach jogged in from shortstop. "Hey kid, throw strikes. This batter has been yours all day."

Julio smiled and nodded his head. Julio paused to gather his thoughts. He took the pitch sign from his brother. The ball whizzed by the batter for a strike.

Jeremy setup for a curve on the outer part of the plate for the next pitch.

"Ball!" the ump yelled.

The Franklin fans gasped while the Cartersville fans cheered.

"C'mon blue, that was strike!" Coach Wilson yelled.

The third pitch was called by Jeremy. Julio acknowledged the sign and went into his windup.

"Strike," the umpired motioned. Our fans roared enthusiastically. It was now down to one pitch. The count was one ball and two strikes.

Jeremy wanted to throw an off speed but the batter had yet to show any ability to hit his brother's fastball. Jeremy looked at the feet of the batter and then signaled for a fastball inside.

Though surprised, Julio determined his brother knew what he was doing. Julio went into his motion and stepped towards home. The ball cut in on the plate. The batter weakly swung and missed.

Game over! We won! The team was number one in the region.

We all rushed into the middle of the field to congratulate each other. Julio pointed at his brother and then towards Alexa who was standing on in the bleachers.

We were number one.

19

Mid May

Mike Williams

It had been several years since we had beaten Cartersville at their place. As you could imagine, the bus ride home was fun. We had won one of the biggest games of the year and Julio was the starting pitcher. Imagine that!

In the back of the bus, I was surrounded by Zach and a few others. We spent the majority of the time telling jokes and teasing each other while Julio sat by himself up front in his normal spot. Looking back, it's too bad we never made an attempt to invite him to the back of the bus. Jeremy sat two seats behind Julio.

Thirty minutes into the ride home, Julio's cell phone buzzed. It was a text from Alexa.

Pizza tonight? You and Jer? My treat!?

Julio sat up. He glanced at Jeremy for his input but he was lost in his music. Julio turned around.

Yep we're game.

Seconds later, Alexa replied back.

Nicole is coming along as well, she knows you're coming.

Julio paused for a moment. He looked out of the bus

and momentarily watched the passing fields. He took a breath.

Sounds good, we look forward to it.

He was such a liar. He may have been looking forward to seeing Alexa, but he definitely wasn't looking forward to seeing Nicole.

Coach Wilson, who was sitting quietly in the front, felt his phone vibrate. It was Jack Winters from the St. Louis organization! Coach looked at his assistant and smiled. "Hey Coach, guess who just sent us a text."

Coach Jacobs shrugged his shoulders.

"Mr. Winters from St. Louis. He is in love with Mike, Julio, and Jeremy." He paused. "Coach, you know we really have a good team... and the scary part is that very few are seniors. Most of these guys will be back next year."

On a side note, I couldn't believe it when Coach told me St. Louis had noticed and was interested in me. I was always told you have to put yourself in a position to be successful through hard work and determination. Those alone don't determine success though. I was also told in sports, as well as life, you'd need a bit of luck along the way. I can't remember who told me that, but I guess they were right.

The bus slowly approached the school after the long

drive from Cartersville. As if a conductor told everyone to stop talking, in unison we all fell silent. In shock, Zach nudged me. I looked at Zach.

The bus driver turned around and looked at the coaches. "Um guys, you need to look outside."

"Well shit," Coach Wilson muttered. "I can't believe some people."

I looked at Zach and then out the window. "Does that say what I think it says?"

Zach nodded his head. "Damn! This isn't good."

Go home! We don't need you here!

was on back the window of Julio's car and

Get out of Franklin

was painted on the side window which faced the bus.

I leaned my head against the back of the seat. "Well shit. You know this pisses me off."

Zach nodded his head. "Yep."

Simultaneously, Zach and I looked up front towards Julio. He sat motionless in his seat.

Coach Wilson looked at Coach Jacobs. "Just when you think it's all good, some idiots. What the hell am I to say to these guys?"

Coach Jacobs shook his head. "I don't know, coach."

Coach Wilson stood up and turned towards us. "Guys, great game today, you have Monday off to rest up for Wednesday's game. Congrats on getting the top seed, the journey is only half over though. It's up to all of you now." He paused. "Needless to say there are some ignorant people out there. We need to stay unified and continue to play together."

Though I didn't disagree with Coach, I was kind of surprised that was all he said, but then again, I'm not sure what I would've said. Actually, I do know what I would've said. I was there. And I said nothing.

Coach Wilson and Coach Jacobs were the first ones off the bus, followed by Julio and Jeremy. One by one the rest of us followed suit. None of us approached Jeremy or Julio. We weren't sure what to say or how to say it. I guess a simple apology would've worked. Then again, I don't know what the hell I would've apologized for. It wasn't like I did anything. I know it pissed me off that two of my teammates were hurt and insulted the way they were.

Coach Jacobs walked towards Julio and Jeremy. He tried to get their attention but it was without much success. Neither one of them looked back towards the bus. Instead, they silently put their gear in the car and drove off. It was all too surreal.

Coach Wilson walked towards the dugout. I imagine he wanted to be alone. While he sat on the bench, he called the police to issue a complaint. The excitement we all felt had all but disappeared like air from a balloon. As for me, I dropped my head and walked to my car, embarrassed and angered.

Once they were in the car, Julio nudged his brother in the side.

Jeremy didn't answer.

Julio nudged him again. "Don't let this bring you down, you did a great job today. Tonight we are going out for pizza with Alexa."

Jeremy looked at his brother. "You said what?"

"Yeah, we're going out for pizza tonight. She texted me while we were on the bus. I wanted to say something to you but you were zoned out."

When Julio pulled into his driveway, he noticed a bucket next to the garage. He took a deep breath. "Get the sponges, I'll fill up the bucket."

Jeremy looked at Julio.

"I said get the sponges. We're not going to make mom do this again. Damn." Julio muttered.

154

After the two scrounged up a sponge and filled up the bucket with water and soap, they began to clean the car windows. Suddenly, Jeremy felt a cold bucket of water on his back followed by a loud laugh. "Gotchu Turkey!" Julio yelled.

Shocked from the sudden splash of water on his back, Jeremy ran off to the side. "Arg!"

Jeremy looked at his brother who was bent over laughing. "Dang that water was cold!" Jeremy bellowed.

"Come on man, let's clean this off," Julio said with a smile.

Jeremy did his best to pretend he was mad, but it was with little success. "Yeah yeah," he said with a smile.

About 30 minutes after they started scrubbing the words off the car, I drove up. Julio and Jeremy looked at the car with reservation until they noticed it was me. I pulled up to the curb and rolled down the passenger window. I was going to get out, but I noticed Julio was walking towards me. I think he was surprised to see a teammate pull up and stop at his house. So, needless to say, he approached my car somewhat nervously.

I leaned towards the passenger window. "I just wanted to say, I'm sorry for what took place back there at the school. You had a great game today. Don't let that ruin your day."

Before Julio could respond, I drove off as quickly as I had arrived. I looked in my rear view mirror and noticed Julio standing on the curb slightly in shock. Whether I was successful or not, I wanted him to know he was part of the team.

Once I was out of sight, Julio turned around and walked towards Jeremy. "Get ready, its pizza time and Alexa's paying!"

They approached Alexa's house. She stood atop the porch with her hands in the air applauding them. Nicole sat in the porch swing smiling. Julio walked towards the porch with Jeremy a few feet behind him. Even though Nicole knew Julio had a brother, she apparently never really noticed him until now and she could not help but think how *un-freshmen* looking he was.

"Guys, you are in for a treat," Alexa said with a smile.

"Ohhh really." Julio said.

"Yep," she answered with a giggle. "Us girls are going to take you out for pizza, so get in my car."

As the four walked towards Alexa's car, Julio looked at Nicole. "So were you at the game today?"

"Yep, it was a good game." She responded shyly.

Julio positioned himself as if he was going to sit in the backseat. "Nahah, no you don't, sit up front," Alexa said as she pointed towards the front seat while she looked at Julio.

Half surprised, Julio looked at Nicole. She looked annoyed. "No, I'll sit in the back. Nicole can sit in the front with you."

Surprisingly, Nicole chimed in. "It's no problem. I'll sit in the back."

Jeremy was nervously excited. I honestly think he was afraid Nicole might start yelling at him, but Nicole was a good looking girl so, of course, he was excited to be sitting next to her. She was one of the better looking girls in the school with her long wavy hair and her athletic figure. She had just one major setback for Julio and Jeremy. She was from Franklin.

The drive to Carbondale went surprisingly smooth. Nicole even seemed to have a good time. As dinner came to a close, Alexa could tell Julio and Jeremy were tired from the long day in the sun.

Alexa looked across the table towards Julio and Jeremy. "Let's get out of here. I can tell you guys are tired."

"Yeah, I bet you two are tired. Dang," Nicole added.

After the four pulled into Alexa's driveway, they piled out of the car and walked towards the porch. "Well, thanks for the pizza, but Jer and I need to get home."

Alexa smiled. "Sounds good, babe."

Julio looked at Nicole. "Well, good night, Nicole. Thanks for the nice evening."

Nicole smiled. "Yep -- And good game today."

After Julio and Jeremy left, Nicole and Alexa sat quietly on the porch.

Nicole, after some time, looked at Alexa. "Why didn't you say anything about the parking lot?"

Alexa shrugged her shoulders. "Tonight was about beating Cartersville."

Nicole sat quietly in the swing. She began to talk, then paused. "What's the scoop on Jeremy?" she asked nervously.

Alexa looked at Nicole and smiled. *It's about time*, Alexa thought to herself.

20

Mid May

Mike Williams

Monday morning quickly arrived. Both Julio and Jeremy walked into the school building like they did every other day, but this time they were greeted by Coach Wilson. He sternly looked at them. Mike Jones, the Athletic Director, stood beside Coach Wilson.

Lightly touching Julio on the shoulder, Coach Wilson asked for him and his brother to follow them to their office. This of course concerned the two, but they knew they had done nothing wrong. They followed the two coaches into Coach Jones' office down in the gym. Upon entering the office, Julio and Jeremy were asked to sit in the chairs next to each other, across from Coach Jones' desk.

"For starters, congrats on beating Cartersville the other day. That was a great victory," Coach Jones said with a smile. "You two do a great job of competing, but you also represented the school with class."

They both smiled in tandem.

Coach Jones took a breath as he leaned forward in his chair. "Boys, we have two reasons for wanting to talk. First of all, how are you about the incident on Saturday? Are you guys okay? Is there anything we can do besides report it to the police and let the principal know? The police are investigating the incident as is the school administration."

Julio leaned forward in his chair. He looked at Jeremy and then his coach. "I think I can speak for Jer. We were both pissed, I'm not going to lie, and I hope the police find the idiots, but this incident is not going to stop us from playing here at Franklin."

Coach Wilson sat back in his chair. He looked at Jeremy and then Julio. "Well please let us know if there is anything we can do to help. That bothered me on Saturday like you wouldn't believe. I took it personally, and, believe it or not, some of your teammates did as well. A few expressed anger with me after you had left."

"Yeah, Williams came by Saturday afternoon."

"Well, just know we're on your side," Coach Jones replied.

"The next topic is a little more positive. Scouts and recruiters have been contacting me. Now Jeremy, you may think this is just a Julio thing, but I'm telling you, we already have some colleges and pro teams asking about you."

Julio looked at Jeremy and then his head coach. "May I

ask who?"

"Sure you can," Coach said with a smile. "Matter of fact, it started on the way home Saturday while we were on the bus and it continued Saturday evening into yesterday. I got a text from a St. Louis scout who is very impressed with both of you, but in the short run, he's interested in you Julio. Southern Illinois is interested, which is of no surprise, but the one that's interesting more than any other is Stanford. You have had an inquiry from Stanford, bud."

Julio sat up. "Stanford, California?"

Coach Wilson laughed. "Yep, that Stanford. I guess one of their coaches saw you last year when you were in Aurora and were impressed. They called your former coach who directed them to Franklin. The next thing you know, he was at the game this past weekend."

Julio proudly smiled.

Coach Jones looked at Jeremy. "Now Jeremy, as we mentioned, this pertains to you also. In the short run, they are following your brother. My recommendation is you pay attention and take it all in. Okay?"

Jeremy replied with a smile. "Yes sir."

Coach Wilson moved in his chair. "We'll write a pass for you guys... Let's finish out the season. We can sit down and talk this summer. We want them to call us and not you. You guys have enough worries."

Both Coach Wilson and Coach Jones stood up. "See you in class Julio," Coach Wilson said with a smile.

After Julio and Jeremy left, Coach Wilson and Coach Jones sat back down in their respective chairs. Coach Wilson looked at his Athletic Director. "Man, the team played great Saturday. I just hope they can remain focused and united as one."

Coach Jones smiled. "Coach, I have seen your teams over the years. This team is scary good and they play together. You may not see it, but I do. The players support Julio and Jeremy. A dumb incident like the one over the weekend will not tear this team apart. If nothing else, it will bring them together."

"I hope you're right, coach," Coach Wilson replied nervously.

"Oh, I am. Just you wait."

Both Julio and Jeremy made it to their classes. Julio approached the door to his first period class and laughed. He was about to "pull an Alexa."

He knocked quietly.

Mr. Wilkins opened the door and allowed Julio in. To

his dismay, Mr. Wilkins didn't even ask for a pass.

He quickly moved to the back.

A piece of folded paper sat on his desk awaiting his arrival. He knew it was from his friend sitting next to him. Alexa grinned which was followed by a tiny wave. He opened the piece of paper -- ?

He quickly jotted down a response.

She opened the note. Her jaw dropped immediately. She couldn't believe what she was reading -- *STANFORD IS INTERESTED IN ME!*

She looked at him and he nodded with a big grin.

The rest of the period moved terribly slow for Alexa. She wanted to ask more questions and Julio could not wait to share more details. Mr. Wilkins finally finished with a few minutes remaining.

Before Alexa could ask or say anything, Jake turned around. "Hey man, great game the other day. Sorry about what was written on your car. That's B.S." he said emphatically.

Julio appreciated Jake for he had been friendly to Julio all year. More so than a lot of us. "Yeah, what can you do? Thanks. Are you ready for the regional tournament?"

Jake rarely played. Unlike Ronald, he knew he wasn't

very good. I think he was just glad to be a part of the team.

Alexa grew more and more restless. "Hello! I hate to interrupt your guy talk."

Jake looked at Alexa and smiled, "What is it, hun?"

Julio laughed. Alexa, who was growingly frustrated, let out a loud groan. Julio tried not to smile. He tapped Jake on the elbow. "Hey bro, I think she's talking to me."

"Oh really? Damn. I thought she was talking to me. I'm sorry."

Alexa dramatically rolled her eyes and flipped her hair.

She looked at Julio and tapped her finger repeatedly on the word *Stanford*.

Finally, Jake turned around.

Julio looked at Alexa. "Yeah...Stanford is asking about me, as is Southern Illinois, and the St. Louis Cardinals."

Jake, turned back around emphatically.

"What!? The Cardinals!?"

"Yep, the Cardinals," Julio replied.

"Stay focused! Stanford, California!?" Alexa blurted.

The bell rang. Julio stood up and looked at Alexa. "Yes," and then looked at Jake. "Yes."

For once both Jake and Alexa were speechless.

Later in the day, Julio sat in Spanish class trying to

gather his thoughts when I sat down in front of him. I turned and looked at Julio with a rather large grin. "I understand you impressed a few scouts the other day?"

Julio smiled.

As you may have guessed, it didn't take long for gossip to spread in our school as small as it was.

A loud voice boomed from the front. "Mr. Williams, please turn around!" yelled Mrs. Megee.

I embarrassingly dipped my head and quickly turned around. Julio could not resist but laugh at me.

Students lingered more and more after school as the temperatures began to warm up. Julio and Jeremy met each other at their normal spot near the front entrance of the school. Without incident, they piled into the car and headed home. Like the rest of us, Julio and Jeremy were glad to have the night off from baseball.

As they entered the side door to the house, their mom and dad greeted them. Mr. James was at the kitchen table sipping a cup of coffee while their mom stood by the sink. Jeremy was the first to enter the house. They threw their school bags down by the kitchen door as if they weighed 50 pounds.

Mr. James took a sip of his coffee and cleared his

throat. "So, I hear there was some good news today, boys?"

Jeremy and Julio looked at each other and then their dad. Both Julio and Jeremy moved towards the two free kitchen chairs. Julio sat down, leaned back, and stretched. "Yeah, Coach called us in this morning. It's pretty cool. Williams is actually being looked at as well. The team is playing well and we are too, so I don't want this to distract us. Coach said we can sit down and talk more once the season is over."

Their dad looked at Jeremy and then Julio. "Alright, just let us know when you boys want to talk about it."

The next few days were uneventful. We won our last game of the season against a much weaker team. Though we didn't play with much intensity, we finished the game strong and no one got hurt.

As we walked off the field, an older man stood by himself dressed in a jacket, tattered pants, and a green hat. The man leaned up against the fence as Coach Wilson passed by. "You have a moment?" the man said in a deep raspy voice.

Coach Wilson looked at him and then Coach Jacobs. Slowly, Coach Wilson walked towards the older gentleman. "Can I help you, sir?"

"Well I don't know, I'm looking for the head coach of this team. Is that you?"

"Yes sir, I am."

"Well sir, you are playing two black boys," the man muttered.

Coach Wilson looked at the stranger. He immediately regretted stopping to converse with the man.

The older man continued. "Well, I just wanted to say you have a good team, and those two boys are good."

"Thanks sir, we seem to think so." Flattered and disturbed by the older man and his compliment, Coach Wilson walked a little faster towards the bus.

21

Late May

Mike Williams

We entered the regional tournament as the number one seed, something that had not been done in a number of years. The evening before our first regional game, against Bensen, Coach Jacobs and Wilson sat in their chairs. Each one had a wad of chew in their mouth. Some of the guys chewed and the Coaches knew it, but I found it disgusting. Sunflower seeds was always more my speed.

Coach Wilson looked at Coach Jacobs.

"Well, who do we want to pitch tomorrow? Julio or Kyle?"

Coach Jacobs didn't respond. Coach Wilson continued.

"We don't want to save Julio and then lose in the semis, but we don't want to throw Julio tomorrow and then throw Kyle in the championship game against an opponent he can't handle."

Julio, Jeremy, and their parents sat at the table and ate dinner and talked baseball.

Down the street, Alexa and Nicole sat on Alexa's porch. The evenings were warming up, but they were still cool enough to need a jacket. Nicole swayed on the porch swing as she sipped from a cup of coffee while Alexa sat on the top step of the porch.

Alexa quietly stared towards the street. The heat from the coffee warmed her hands.

"Is something bothering you?" Nicole asked curiously.

Alexa leaned her head against the porch post. "Nah, I just have a lot on my mind right now."

"You wanna talk about whatever is bothering you?"

Alexa smiled. "Now Nicole...You haven't been the most supportive."

Nicole positioned herself against the armrest of the swing. "I don't disagree with you, but..."

Alexa continued. "I guess I'm just scared. I'm really into Julio. I mean, what if he decides to go someplace to play ball and we're really far apart and he forgets about me?"

"Alexa, don't be an idiot. For starters, that boy is into YOU. Yeah, he loves baseball, and damn that boy is good, but come on!"

"You think he likes me? I mean our dates have been pretty laid back."

Nicole rolled her eyes. "Do you hear what you're saying?! Think about where you live! He doesn't have much of a choice but to take things slow. I mean… Franklin doesn't exactly have the most open minded people."

"So what should I do then?"

"So let me get this straight. You're asking me what you should do? Right? Do you remember me telling you back at Christmas to stay away from him?"

Alexa was visibly aggravated. "Yes."

Nicole continued. "Did I not tell you stay away from him in the fall?"

"Yes," Alexa replied as if she was defeated.

"If you let him go because of me you are a damn idiot."

Alexa looked at Nicole. A tear ran down her cheek from the corner of her left eye.

Nicole continued, "Do you hear me!?" as she pointed her finger at Alexa.

Alexa nodded shyly. "Yep and thanks Nicole, I don't know what I would do without you!"

Nicole laughed. "Yep you'd be no one around here without me."

Thursday quickly arrived. Julio and Jeremy drove to school like every other day, with one slight difference. Julio didn't know which game he was going to be asked to pitch.

They pulled into their space. Off to the left was Nicole

who was laughing with Janet. Nicole was becoming tougher for Julio to read.

In unison, Jeremy and Julio got out of the car. Julio tried to keep from making eye contact with the two girls. Nicole felt conflicted when she noticed Julio and Jeremy. She tried not to look at them, but she couldn't help it.

She flipped her hair to her side. Nicole looked at Julio and followed with a glancing smile at Jeremy. Julio acknowledged her with a polite smile. Jeremy didn't know what to do. A junior, an attractive one at that, was acknowledging him.

Janet, confused, watched the exchange between Nicole and *the two field hands.*

"Good luck tonight guys," Nicole said shyly.

Julio and Jeremy looked at each other. "Thanks, hope you're coming," Julio replied.

"Oh, definitely!"

Julio and Jeremy noticed Coach Wilson was standing by himself as they approached the school doors. Julio looked at Jeremy and slyly nudged him on the arm.

Jeremy nodded his head, smiled, and began to walk away. "I'll talk to you later. Let's kick some butt tonight," Jeremy added confidently.

Julio continued to walk towards his coach.

"Well, you ready to shut down Bensen tonight?"

Julio smiled. "Just give me the ball coach and I'll do my best."

The day breezed by. Of course little to no learning took place for me so I'm sure Julio was no different. Even when Alexa flirted with him he struggled to flirt back.

Game time finally came. We were amazingly focused considering our opponent. Bensen made it to the semis by upsetting teams on the way, so they were a huge underdog. Coach Wilson did his best to remind us Bensen won two games to get to the semis, and though Bensen was the underdog, we still had to win the game and not give it away. Thankfully, Bensen's pitching was depleted because they used their best two pitchers to advance to the semi-finals.

As expected, we quickly scored on Bensen and Julio made quick work of the team. The game was over in five innings with us winning 12-0. Julio threw just four innings which was the icing on the cake because it meant he would be able to throw in the championship game if needed.

Saturday, the day of the championship game, was a beautiful sunny day. Not a cloud could be seen in the sky and the temperatures were in the low 70s. It was definitely short sleeve weather. By the time the game started, the bleachers were full on each side as if the whole town had come to support us. Like every other time, Julio's parents sat as far down as they could on the right field line. Alexa joined them. She rested on her blanket she had grown to enjoy throughout the season.

The game started off quietly. Neither team scored through three innings, but we did have our chance several times. We just couldn't hit the ball at the right time. Kyle Whitten was throwing his best game to date. His fastball kept Carbondale off balance and his curve was unhittable.

In the fourth inning, with one man on base, Zach walked confidently to the plate. He stepped into the batter's box and looked towards his coach at third. Coach Wilson gave Zach and the runner on first the hit and run sign.

The pitcher motioned home. Darrin, the runner on first, took off towards second. Running towards second, Darrin peeked out of the corner of his left eye towards home to see if Zach was going to hit the ball. The pitch couldn't have been in a better spot for Zach. He stepped towards the ball and swung his bat. The ball jumped off his bat and lined towards right field. We were quickly up 2-0 by the time it was all said and done.

In the fifth and sixth innings, Carbondale battled back to tie the game up at two. We were unable to answer in the bottom of the sixth inning. The game remained tied into the seventh.

Coach Wilson looked at Coach Jacobs in between the fifth and sixth innings. "I'm so glad we only used Julio for four innings Thursday."

Coach Jacobs smiled. "Yeah I know, thank God."

During the sixth inning while we were up to bat, Coach looked at Julio. "You are throwing next inning. Get loosened up."

Displeased, Kyle threw down his glove in disgust.

Zach saw Kyle throw down his glove. "Dude buck up, we got this game. Julio's the man."

Julio walked slowly towards the mound at the top of the seventh inning. After he threw his warmup pitches, Jeremy turned towards the umpire to call timeout. He walked to the mound with his mask in hand and quickly ran through the pitching signs with his brother.

As Jeremy approached home, he looked at the umpire. "Man, my brother is pissed," he said with a smile. "I pity the fool who will try to hit him." Of course, Jeremy said it loud enough so the batter could hear him.

On que, Julio made quick work of the next three batters. Many of the fans stood up in support as the inning came to a close, but a few idiots refused to stand up and cheer. I guess they were disgusted Julio came in to relieve Kyle.

It was now our chance to win the game. As luck would have it, the top of the lineup was due up. Though Zach, Eric, Julio, and I had struggled all day long, we all had hit the ball well. Not only were we good hitters, but we were also home run threats.

Zach approached home plate. He looked at Coach Wilson who was at third and followed with a glance into the dugout. Zach took a breath and let the bat swing lightly as he relaxed into his stance in the batter's box.

The pitcher went into his motion and threw the ball home. Zach noticed the seams on the ball as it spun towards him. His hands and bat exploded towards the ball. The ball bounced off his bat and flew towards left field. As soon as it was hit, Zach knew it was home run!

He threw his hands into the air as he ran down the first base line. With great enthusiasm, everyone in the dugout ran out to greet him as he sprinted around the bases. He finally ran towards home. We were the regional champs! The next stop would be the sectionals.

22

Late May

Mike Williams

The bus rumbled through the countryside towards Cartersville, the home of the sectional championship. The previous Saturday, Marion High lost to Shawneeville High in extra innings. Thankfully, we beat Pikesville High rather decisively. The bus ride to Cartersville was pretty quiet except for the few idiots who didn't know when to shut up. Of course, they were primarily freshmen. Most of us sat and listened to the music of our choice on our various devices.

Midway through the ride, Zach poked me in the side. I looked at him rather irritatingly. He smiled and pointed out the back window.

I couldn't believe it! A long stretch of cars extended behind our bus for a good distance. I looked at Zach. "Are those Franklin fans?"

He smiled. "Crazy, huh?"

Kyle, Kory, Ronald and a few others must have heard us because they turned around to check out the excitement. It was sight to see and one of those times I was proud to be from Franklin.

Away from the commotion, Julio sat quietly in his seat and stared at the seat in front of him while he listened to his music.

Behind Julio sat Jeremy. His body was spread across two seats. Yeah, he was one relaxed cat. I wished I could've been as relaxed as he was. Darn Freshmen!

The bus finally reached Cartersville. The other team was already on the field loosening up. Music boomed from the speakers. Even though they had a farther distance to travel, many of the fans from Shawneeville were already in the bleachers.

Zach noticed the large crowd already in the bleachers. He nudged me with his elbow. "Dang, will you look at that. Don't they have a life?"

I looked at Zach and laughed.

"Dude, did you not see the cars behind us?"

Zach smiled. "Point taken."

The town of Shawneeville is located in the southeastern part of the state along the Ohio River. Like Franklin, it's a small rural community of farmers and small business owners who took pride in their baseball. Sadly, since the 80s, the population has dwindled because the coal mines in the area had shut down which hurt the town immensely.

I looked at Zach and smiled. "Zach, this game is going to be a battle."

"Yeah, but we have a better team than they do," Zach added confidently.

"Do we?" Sadly, I didn't have the confidence Zach had.

The bus finally rolled to a stop near the right field fence line. We quickly moved about the bus. As we gathered our equipment not a word was spoken.

Coach Wilson stood up in the middle of the aisle in the front of the bus. He waited until everyone stopped moving around. "Let's kick some butt, boys," he said with his fists in the air. Of course that got us excited. I think I could've eaten nails at that point.

Julio nudged Jeremy. "Look bro, soak it in. This will be fun."

Jeremy looked at Julio and smiled half-heartedly.

On the hill beyond the left field wall were numerous fans for both teams. They were busily grilling food and enjoying life. As much as I'd like to think they came to watch a great game, I wonder if we were just an excuse to grill out.

We filed into the dugout one by one. Normally we wore our blue tops with the white pants, but we voted to wear the all blue uniform. Heck, we rarely wore all blue, but, like the other guys, I thought it looked pretty cool. Shawneeville, on the other hand, wore white with red pinstripes. Kind of boring if you ask me.

The Shawneeville players seemed bigger. Some of them actually looked like grown men who had not shaved for a week. At one point I overheard someone from our team ask, "Geeze, are those guys Paul Bunyan's kids?"

Shawneeville's pitcher was Jake Young, a tall junior lefty. Like the rest of the team he was tall and I'm willing to bet he never missed a meal in his life.

The one thing we had going for us outside of Julio pitching is that we had played on this field before. We weren't as mesmerized by the little things like the speakers in the outfield, the signs, and the loud music which blasted throughout the field.

As game time approached, Julio and Jeremy slowly made their way down the right field line towards the corner to stretch and loosen up. I bet Julio was glad to be wearing sleeves under his jersey, because a slight breeze blew from right field towards left field.

Once Julio was loose, he and Jeremy made their way quietly back to the dugout.

Julio looked towards the outfield as he leaned up against the railing. He was standing next to me.

"This is so cool."

"Yes it is," I responded.

Julio glanced towards the bleachers and noticed Alexa. Of course, she stood out from everyone else. Alexa, Nicole, and a few others were dressed in blue and had an "F" painted on their cheeks with blue eye shadow, which I thought was a nice touch. Alexa set herself apart from the others by wearing blue heels.

A little restless, Julio walked from one end of the dugout to the other. He noticed Zach who was playing with his glove. Zach stopped what he was doing and smiled. "Are you ready to kick some butt?"

Julio nodded. "Do your thing out there. We'll need you."

When the National Anthem came to a close, the fans in the outfield honked their horns.

Julio looked at Jeremy. "Are you ready bro?"

Jeremy held his fist up for Julio to bump.

Julio put his right arm around his little brother.

"Let's have some fun today. I wouldn't want anyone else behind the plate. Just do what you have been doing all year."

In the stands, Alexa and Nicole stood on the bleachers and clapped and chanted "Franklin" over and over again along with many of the students. The students took over the far end of the bleachers. The rows were filled with students dressed in blue and their enthusiasm was undeniable.

Prior to taking the field, we as a team circled up outside of our dugout with Coach Wilson in the middle. After giving a bunch of us high fives, he looked at Julio.

"Go after these guys. You're our man."

Coach Wilson continued. "Guys...just play within yourselves. Don't try to make the big play, let it come and we'll win." He extended his arm into the air. We, as a team, followed suit.

Coach Wilson belted out, "FRANKLIN!"

In response we yelled "FRANKLIN!"

Since we were the home team, our defense sprinted onto the field. The fans continued to chant our name. The outfielders reached their positions and were greeted with honking horns and boos from the opposing fans.

Eric waved to a few of the fans he recognized once he reached his position in centerfield. He smiled when the fans from Shawneeville began to yell at him. He acknowledged them with a wave as well. Thankfully, he didn't give them a one finger wave. That wouldn't have been good.

Any nervousness Jeremy may have felt disappeared rather quickly as he warmed up his brother. The last pitch zinged home and made a loud pop when it hit Jeremy's glove. I even heard it at third base.

After Jeremy's hard warm-up throw to second, the infield tossed the ball around the infield. Julio held his glove up in anticipation of a soft toss from me. Instead, I slowly walked towards Julio. When I finally reached the mound I flipped him the ball. "Go after these guys. We got your back."

Julio gathered himself before he stepped up onto the mound. After he took a deep breath, he stepped into his windup. The ball zipped towards home, but it did not cut in on the batter liked Julio hoped. In one pitch, Shawneeville was up by one as the ball drifted over the left field wall.

The crowd erupted on the Shawneeville side as the batter rounded third and headed towards home. Our fans sat in silence, shocked by the instant score change.

Several students belittled Julio which caused Alexa to turn around in disgust. Her lips quivered with anger. Though she wanted to say something she held her tongue. It's not like it would have done any good.

Julio received a ball from the umpire as the batter ran around the bases. When the batter crossed home, Julio looked away in angrily and took a deep breath. Jeremy stood behind home plate. He shrugged his shoulders when Julio glanced his way.

The next batter up was a tall lefty. Unlike the first pitch of the game, the batter swung and missed the first pitch he saw. The coaches stood in the dugout and looked at each other.

"Looks like he has his rhythm back." Coach Wilson muttered to himself.

The batter worked the count to two balls and one strike. Julio tried to sneak a curve by the batter on the outer part of the plate. Instead, batter drove the ball hard to left field. Two back to back hard hit balls. Crap!

"This isn't how we hoped to start."

"Looks like these guys have come to play," Coach Jacobs replied.

The next two batters grounded out to me at third base. With a runner on second and two outs, Julio stepped onto the mound. The batter due up was a tall hard hitting right hander. Julio took a breath as he looked towards home.

He took the sign from his brother, stepped into his position and paused. The pitch left Julio's hand and drifted over the middle of the plate. The batter's eyes widened.

SMACK!

The ball zipped over me into leftfield.

As soon as the ball left the bat, Julio looked down in disgust and thought *shit another homer*.

All of the fans jumped to their feet. The players from each bench ran to the edge of their respective dugouts to watch the ball sail into the outfield. The ball drifted and drifted. As it neared the wall, the ball slowly came down into Darrin's glove who was camped under the ball at the wall in left field. Thankfully, the inning was finally over.

Thank God! I thought to myself. I could only imagine what Julio was thinking.

Coach Wilson glanced at his assistant. "Whew, that was close."

Jeremy was a lot more optimistic. He greeted his brother. "Just a long fly out, no biggie."

Julio walked past Jeremy with his head down. This was by far the worst start Julio had completed all year.

Coach Wilson stood on the edge of the grass with his

hands on his hips. Julio didn't realize his coach was in front of him. Coach reached out and stopped Julio by the arm and looked Julio in the eyes.

"You need to bear down and go after these turkeys. Be a pitcher, not a thrower!"

Julio looked at Coach. "Yes sir."

Coach then looked at Jeremy. "Stop acting like a freshman and make the right calls back there, you're better than this!"

Surprised, Jeremy replied rather meekly, "Yes sir."

I personally think Coach just needed to yell at someone and Jeremy happened to be the closest one there to yell at.

The breeze had come to a halt as the clouds rolled in to hide the sun. Julio finally settled in. The next few innings he only allowed a smattering of hits. Offensively, we couldn't hit the damn ball. As a result, we had failed to score any runs through five innings.

The game slipped into the sixth inning. Shawneeville's lead was still just one. Our fans were growing restless with each passing out while the fans for Shawneeville were growing more and more vocal. Heck, every time an out was made, the Shawneeville fans honked their horns in the outfield which was so damn aggravating.

Coach Wilson approached Julio in between the fifth and sixth innings. "How do you feel? Can you go into the sixth inning?"

Julio looked at Coach Wilson. "Yeah, I'm fine."

"Good, because it's yours."

Julio stepped up onto the mound at the beginning of the sixth inning. Even though he was tired, he definitely wasn't going to tell Coach nor was he going to say anything to Jeremy. He adjusted his hat and breathed in slowly.

Coach Wilson stood on the edge of the dugout next to Coach Jacobs. "Well...It's the top of the lineup so let's hope he can get out of the inning."

The lead-off batter approached the batter's box. Julio and Jeremy looked at each other. Jeremy motioned down with his glove and hands.

Jeremy called for the first pitch to be up and away. Strike one, surprising the batter who was looking for a low pitch. The second pitch, was called: up and away again. Again, the batter was late. Strike two. With two strikes on the batter, Jeremy called for a changeup low and away. Confident in Jeremy's decision, Julio threw a changeup low and away. Strike three. The batter was out after a weak attempt at the ball.

The next batter went down like a pile of bricks on three pitches as well. Two outs.

As the third batter stepped to the plate, fans on both sides stood on their feet. The count was quickly two balls and two strikes. The last thing Julio wanted to allow was a runner on base with two outs. Julio stepped behind the rubber and looked around. He looked at Zach and then me over at third. I smiled and gave him a thumbs up.

Julio walked up onto the mound. Jeremy looked into the dugout and then at Julio. He put down one finger and tapped his right leg signaling for a fastball outside. Julio stepped into his motion. The ball hit the outer part of the plate. Strike three!

As soon as the inning finished, Coach Wilson motioned for his reliever, Kory, to go get loosened up.

Julio walked up to Coach Wilson. "You are not taking me out, Coach. I feel good."

Coach guided Julio by the arm to the side of the dugout. "Relax", Coach said in a deep voice. "You're going in next inning, but if I see any signs of being tired, you're out. You understand me?"

Julio smiled. "Yes sir."

Again, we were unable to score any runs. Frustratingly,

we couldn't buy a hit. No matter how hard we hit the ball, the Shawneeville players seemed to be there to field it.

Julio made his way back out towards the mound. The Shawneeville team looked on with amazement as Julio took the mound in the seventh inning. They probably hadn't seen this hard of a thrower go this long in a game.

Alexa couldn't decide whether she wanted to stand up or sit down. The whole time Nicole did her best to relax her best friend.

In the press box sat two scouts, one from St. Louis and one from San Francisco. Behind the scouts were three college recruiters. One was from Southern Illinois while the other two were from Stanford and Ohio State.

Julio was determined to make quick work of the batters and he did. The last out was a fly to centerfield. Julio had gone seven innings and allowed only one run. Sadly, it was the first pitch of the game.

It was now do or die for our team. The bottom of the lineup was due up for us which was definitely not ideal.

Jeremy was the first batter up. He grounded out to second on the first pitch. The next batter up was Darrin, our left fielder and senior, who had struggled all game as well. He struck out on four pitches. With two outs, Eric was due up.

As he approached home plate, the fans on each side stood up to cheer. The players in each dugout came to the edge of their respective dugouts.

Alexa stood quietly on the edge of the bleachers. Nicole did her best to comfort her friend but she had little success. The James parents sat quietly down the right field line away from the other fans. Not a word was spoken between the two.

Eric stepped into the batter's box. He took a number of deep breaths. *Don't be the last out* he thought to himself.

The first pitch was up and in. Ball one. The Shawneeville crowd grunted loudly. The Franklin High fans erupted with a loud cheer. The next pitch was low and away. Ball two. Again, the Shawneeville fans groaned while our fans cheered enthusiastically. The count was now two balls and no strikes.

Eric stepped out of the box. The third pitch was thrown down the middle of the plate. Eric's eyes widened.

CLANK!

The ball bounced off his bat and drifted towards left field. As Eric sprinted down the baseline, he watched the ball. In disgust, the opposing pitcher dropped his head.

The ball continued to drift towards the wall. The left fielder ran to the edge of the wall. Eric raised his arms in the air with excitement. Then, his heart was ripped out of him. The ball was caught at the base of the wall. The game was over.

The left fielder looked in his glove for confirmation. The Shawneeville team paused and then exploded out of the dugout for they were going to the state championship. Our season was done.

After shaking hands with the Shawneeville players Julio sat at the end of the dugout by the entrance with his head down. He noticed a pair of shoes saddle up next to him. He looked up. Zach stood over him.

Zach reached his right hand out towards Julio. "Hey, keep your head up. Without you and your brother, we wouldn't be here. We'll get them next year. We didn't help you out today, sorry." Zach walked out of the dugout before Julio had a chance to reply.

23

Mike Williams

Even though a week had passed since the sectional loss to Shawneeville, it still stung. Across town Julio laid quietly on his bed. A cool breeze whisked into his room. The downstairs phone rang.

After a half-hour, Julio and Jeremy heard a knock on the door.

"Boys, can I come in?" Their dad asked.

Julio and Jeremy looked at each other rather perplexed. Julio shrugged his shoulders and Jeremy followed suit.

"Sure!" Julio yelled out.

Mr. James walked in and sat down in the desk chair across from Julio who was sitting up on his bed. He glanced at Julio and smiled.

"That was the Stanford coach a few minutes ago on the phone."

Julio immediately sat up. "What did he want?"

"Well, apparently they would love for you to come to Stanford for a visit."

Julio couldn't believe what he was hearing. "No way! You can't be serious!"

Questions immediately ran through his head: *Do they want me as a pitcher? What game did they see me in? Didn't they see me give up that homer? Oh crap, what will Alexa think?*

His dad continued. "I thought we could fly out to California, so you could check out the campus." He paused. "Maybe if you're interested you'd want to take a friend as well?"

Mr. James paused. He looked at Jeremy and smiled. "We didn't take a vacation last year either."

"A friend?" Julio asked curiously.

Mr. James laughed. "Yep, a friend. I thought maybe Alexa would like to go and visit the campus as well. If it was fine with her parents, of course."

"Ohhhh, a girl?" Jeremy added jokingly.

Julio launched his pillow across the room at his younger brother in disgust.

"I thought we'd fly out to San Francisco, stay a few days in Palo Alto where Stanford is located, maybe catch a Giants game, and visit San Francisco some. How does that sound?"

"So... should I ask Alexa?" Julio asked curiously.

His dad paused. "How about you give me her home number. I'll call her parents and talk to them. That way they know everything is fine and they can ask me any questions they may have."

Mr. James stood up and tapped Julio's leg. He looked at Jeremy and then back towards Julio. "Get me her number as soon as you can. The sooner the better."

Julio looked at his dad. "Yes sir."

Julio quickly showered, or at least pretended to shower. He was hardly in the shower long enough to get wet. He quickly moved around the room like some superhero getting dressed. Jeremy kept finding ways to get in Julio's way. Not on purpose of course.

After throwing on a t-shirt and shorts, Julio galloped down the stairs as if a herd of wild buffalo were on the loose. His mom and dad were at the kitchen table with their computer when he rushed in.

"Son? Where are you going in such a hurry?" his mom asked sarcastically.

"Oh, I'm just heading over to Alexa's to get her home number for you guys."

"Well, why don't you just call her?" she asked with a smile.

Julio shyly smiled and ran out the door as if his pants were on fire.

The door swung shut behind him. His dad yelled at him. "Drive safe, son!"

Julio raised his hand half-heartedly and waved back at his dad. He didn't have time for small talk.

Minutes later, Julio was in Alexa's driveway. When Julio pulled up, Alexa was on the porch sipping her coffee. She perked up and smiled when she noticed his car.

She clearly didn't expect him, otherwise she would've taken the time to look *presentable.*

He walked up the porch steps and sat down on the swing. "Can I sit here?" he asked as he moved her feet to the side.

Alexa smiled. "So, what's up dude?"

"Well, my family is going to California so I can visit Stanford. My parents were curious if you'd want to go with?"

She nearly spit up her coffee she was so surprised.

Julio continued. "Yeah, my parents want to be able to call your parents and talk to them as opposed to going back and forth between us. Assuming you want to go."

Alexa smiled. "Do you want me to go?"

"Of course I do."

"Well then, I'll give you my parents' number and I won't say a word to them until your parents talk to them."

She took another sip of her coffee as Julio texted his parents her number. "So why Stanford?"

He shrugged his shoulders. "Their coach wants me to come out for a campus visit and my dad thought this would be a great chance to go visit San Francisco for vacation."

She smiled. "I could handle visiting California for a few days."

The phone rang inside the house. They immediately moved into eavesdrop mode. Much to their disappointment, neither Alexa nor Julio could make out what her mom said while she was on the phone. After nearly ten minutes Julio's phone buzzed.

He noticed it was a message from his dad. ***She's going!***

Just about the time Julio received his text message from his dad, Alexa's mom stepped outside. Like her daughter, she was holding a cup of coffee.

I guess Apples don't fall far from the tree.

She stood in the doorway with a smirk on her face. "I

guess you've been invited to go to California with the James'. Do you want to go?"

"Mom, are you serious? Do I get to go?"

"Of course you do. I know the James' will keep an eye on you. I'm not sure about this young man next to you though. He seems to be trouble." She winked at Julio.

"Eek!" Alexa shrieked, which caused her mom and Julio to cringe momentarily. "We're going to Cali, to Cali, to Cali!" she chanted enthusiastically.

Mrs. Sherman glanced at Julio. "So tell me about why you're visiting Stanford?"

"Well ma'am, Stanford wants me to visit the campus I guess."

"Oh wow! Are there any other teams looking at you?"

"Yes ma'am. Southern Illinois is interested in me as are a couple of pro teams. I was told St. Louis has talked to Coach about me several times. I know a few other schools have looked at me, but that's all I know."

Mrs. Sherman stood in the doorway with her mouth open. "Did you say professional teams?" She looked at Julio and then Alexa. "Alexa, you better not let this young man go!"

"Mom be quiet, geeze!" Alexa yelled out.

24

Mid June

Mike Williams

Alexa sat in her seat which looked out at the city of San Francisco. In the distance, she could see the ocean and mountains which made her smile. She was back in California again! She looked at Julio, who was next to her.

"What?" Julio asked curiously.

"Oh, I am just excited to be here. Thanks for the invitation." She laid her head on his shoulder while she continued to smile.

"Don't thank me, thank my dad."

After several minutes, the plane finally landed. Once off the plane, they made their way to the baggage claim. They gathered their bags and made their way outside where they were immediately greeted by the cool San Francisco air.

The family drove down the coast of California towards Palo Alto where Stanford was located. Though the drive took an hour, it seemed much quicker.

"Hey, look!" Alexa yelled as she pointed towards a sign on the side of the road which read **Coming this**

Fall: Stanford Football. Gleefully, she nudged Julio. She quickly whipped out her phone, pointed it towards the sign, and clicked.

"Wow, look at those trees. Those pines are beautiful." Mrs. James added as she stared out the car window.

Everyone except for Mr. James looked enthusiastically to the left to glance at the trees.

Minutes later, they veered off of Interstate 280. "We're here guys!" Mr. James exclaimed as he pulled the car into the hotel parking lot.

"Hey, look! There's a pool." Alexa exclaimed gleefully. "I'm glad I brought my bikini."

Mrs. James turned around and smiled. "Honey, don't you think it will be too cool to swim?"

Alexa grinned. "Oh no, it's never too cool to go swimming."

Alexa looked to her right and noticed Julio was dozing off. "Wake up you goober. I mean, if anyone should be tired it's me. I got up at four this morning."

Julio grunted.

Mr. James exited from the front of the hotel with the keys to the two rooms in his hand. He looked at Alexa. "You'll be rooming with my wonderful wife. She shouldn't be too bad."

"Yeah, at least I don't snore," she said as she poked her husband in the side. "Did you bring your earplugs, boys?" she asked jokingly.

Alexa smiled.

Julio looked at Jeremy. "Well, it looks like we got the raw end of this deal."

The rest of the afternoon went by quickly. Before long, night had set in. Everyone except for Mrs. James woke up before their alarm. Even Mr. James woke up early which caught everyone by surprise. After the troop had their breakfast, they piled into the car. Of course, Julio and Jeremy fought over who would sit where. All Alexa wanted to do was sit by Julio, so it did not matter to her. Unknowingly to her, Julio and Jeremy had determined Alexa would sit in the middle no matter what. She looked like a blonde sardine.

It was obvious the University of Stanford made up a large part of the town. Everywhere they looked they saw signs for the school.

After several lefts and rights, they approached something out of a movie. The stadium was not as large as the football stadium, but it was biggest baseball field he had ever seen, other than the professional stadiums he had been to. There was a large parking lot, which was empty at the time. Mr. James drove around to the back of the stadium where in big letters there was a sign which read **WELCOME TO STANFORD**.

Before their dad turned off the ignition to the car, Julio and Jeremy piled out of the vehicle as if they were jumping from a bomb. Alexa looked to her left and then to her right. She threw her hands in the air and smiled.

"At least they left the door open for me."

"Man, that is one cool view," Julio mumbled under his breath as he looked towards the mountains with the stadium directly in front of him.

"Yep," Jeremy replied.

Alexa finally worked her way out of the car. She slinked up next to Julio and slid her arm around him. He looked down and smiled at her as he put his arm around her.

She leaned in tight. "So, what do you think?"

"I love this!" He replied followed with a kiss on the lips.

The family, in silent amazement, walked along the stadium. Alexa looked to her right and noticed a man off in the distance. She nudged Julio. About the same time, his parents noticed the same man who was wearing a Stanford polo shirt with Khaki pants.

"So you must be Julio James?" the man said with a smile as he approached the group with an outstretched hand. "I'm Paul Walker, the head Coach."

The man must have been nearly 50 with blue eyes, greyish hair, and stood about 5'10." He shook Julio's hand first, then looked at Alexa and smiled. "I have a daughter who looks just like you." Alexa smiled and blushed all at once. He looked at Julio's parents. "Nice to meet you. You must be his parents."

He looked at Jeremy. "You must be Jeremy. I've heard a lot about you."

Jeremy proudly smiled.

Coach Walker looked at Julio. Alexa unleashed her arm from Julio's. "You and your family want to take a little walk?"

Julio smiled. "Sure."

Coach Walker and Julio walked through the stadium and talked about the campus and the facilities. His dad walked behind them and asked questions when he felt it was needed. At one point, Coach Walker took them down to the dugout.

After a long conversation with Julio and his parents, he

looked at Alexa. "So where are you looking to go to school?"

She looked at Julio and then Julio's parents. "Well sir, I'm actually from California and I've always wanted to return here, but my dad teaches at Southern Illinois. So, I don't really know."

Coach Walker nudged Julio. "Did you hear her? She's wants to live in California." He paused momentarily. "I am willing to bet we will have two Cardinals going to school here."

Coach Walker looked at his parents and then Julio. "Do you have any more questions?"

Julio looked at his dad and then Coach Walker. "No sir."

Coach smiled. "Terrific. Well take a look at the campus and don't hesitate to contact my offices if you have any more questions."

The family quietly walked back to the car. Minutes later they were at one of the many small parking lots on campus. Julio and Alexa, hand in hand, slowly separated from everyone else.

Alexa looked at Julio. "I'm excited for you."

Julio squeezed her hand.

"I can't get over how cool this campus looks," she added.

Julio's mom somehow overheard her. "I know, this campus is so pretty. I love the architecture."

Students buzzed by on their bikes as if they were walking in slow motion.

Before they had realized it, noon was upon them.

"Is anyone hungry?" Mr. James asked as he moved to the side so a biker could pass by.

In synchronization the family all responded, "I am."

They came upon a restaurant called *The Sandwich Shop* which overlooked the campus. After they bought their sandwiches, they found a spot and sat down. You would have thought they hadn't eaten in days.

"So what do you think?"

Mr. James looked at Julio. "About what? The school?"

"Yep."

"This is a great school. If you want to come here we will do whatever is needed to make that happen."

Julio didn't answer. Instead, he sat quietly in his seat and ate his sandwich.

"It's a beautiful campus," his mom added.

Julio glanced below and noticed the students frantically move from one place to another.

Alexa looked out from her seat. "Oh wow, look! There's

a park over there. Cool! They are playing frisbee. I miss that!" She exclaimed.

Always a fan of a good sandwich, Mr James continued to devour his. Julio still hadn't answered his dad's question. "It doesn't matter what we think, do you want to go here? If it was my decision, this school would be on my shortlist, but it's up to you." Mr. James went back to enjoying his sandwich.

Julio leaned back in his chair. For once in his life, he wasn't very hungry. He looked out onto the campus from where he sat. Alexa reached out and tugged at his hand and smiled. He continued to stare into the distance.

Mr. James took his last bite and sat back in his chair. He looked at his wife who happened to be in the sun. "You look amazing today, hun."

Caught off guard, Mrs. James smiled. "Oh thanks!"

Mr. James looked at Alexa. "So what's your take? Do you like this school?

"Sir, I'm going to apply here when I get home."

"Why's that?" Mr. James asked.

"I'm just in love with this campus. I honestly want to get out of Southern Illinois, as well, sir."

"I can understand that, hun," Mrs. James added.

Mr. James took a sip of his drink. "So who wants to see the Giants tonight?"

Everyone looked at him dumbfounded and shocked. "I have tickets for the Giants game tonight!"

"Oh cool!" Alexa belted. "I've never been to a game outside of St. Louis."

Jeremy and Julio happily looked at each other.

Around mid-afternoon they headed towards San Francisco to watch some baseball. As the game wore on, Julio imagined himself playing for the Giants. He actually liked that thought.

By the seventh inning the Giants were well behind, so the James family decided to head back to Palo Alto. The car drive home was a quiet one since everyone was tired from the long, exciting day. Julio's head rested against the back of the car seat. He was barely able to keep his eyes open. Alexa sat next to him with her head rest against Julio's side. From time to time she would stroke his arm.

A grin worked its way across Alexa's face as she rested her head on Julio. *I'm going to Stanford no matter what* she thought.

25

Late June

Mike Williams

Julio and his dad approached Franklin High school. The campus was empty except for a few teachers and administrators. Julio was already dripping in sweat and it was only 10 in the morning; a far cry from the coast of California.

Both Julio and his dad walked into the school and were immediately greeted by both coaches. Coach Jacobs wanted to participate in the meeting because he had played minor league baseball and was familiar with the recruiting process. Actually, a week earlier, I had met with the coaches as well with my dad.

Coach Wilson extended his hand. "Morning guys."

After a short greeting, Coach Wilson led them down to his office just off the gym.

Coach Wilson looked at Julio. "So how was it?"

"I liked it."

"Yeah, I figured you would," Coach added.

As they approached the office, Julio looked around. "Man, this place is quiet."

Both coaches smiled. "Yes it is," added Coach Wilson.

After a minute's walk, they finally reached the office. As they entered the office, Coach Wilson directed Julio and his dad to the two empty chairs in front of the desk. Coach Jacobs followed Julio and Mr. James into the office. Coach Wilson leaned back in his chair and put his feet up on the desk as if he did not have a care in the world. This was not the Coach Julio was used to talking to.

Coach paused momentarily. "I wanted you to come in this morning with your dad so we could talk about the trip. Other schools have been calling in the last few weeks as well." He paused. "And some professional teams have been in communication.

Before Julio could respond, Coach Jacobs cut into the conversation. "We can talk about the teams who are calling you, but it comes down to what you want to do. Do you want to play college ball or would you rather take a shot at being drafted."

Julio shyly smiled. "I think I would prefer to play college ball, develop my skills, and then take a shot at going pro."

Coach Jacobs pondered Julio's answer. "What if you go to college, get injured, and can't play pro?"

"Well sir," Julio responded, "a degree can go with me

no matter what happens to me in baseball."

Coach Jacobs challenged Julio's decision even more. "What if you're able to get a clause in your contract, if signed by a professional team, they would pay for your schooling."

"Yeah, I still want to play college."

Coach Wilson looked at his dad. "Well I wouldn't rule out anything just yet. Keep your options open."

"What if I signed a letter of intent?"

"I would wait on that," added Coach Wilson. "We don't want your stock to be driven down. There's no hurry."

"It kind of depends who drafts me also, Coach," Julio added.

Coach Jacobs smiled. "Yeah, that makes sense."

Coach Wilson looked at Julio. "I want you to know, whatever you decide, we'll support you, but we want the best for you. We also want you to be happy with your choice. Did you like Stanford enough to go there?"

Julio smiled. "Loved it!"

"Well this is what you need to do then," Coach continued, "you need to call up Stanford and ask what they are willing to offer and feel free to ask any questions you need to ask. Food, lodging, anything. If that's where you want to go, great. It's a great school. You just need to be informed."

Mr. James, who had been quiet most of the meeting looked at Coach Wilson. "What do you think? Should he play college or professional ball?"

Coach Jacobs looked at Julio's dad. "Sir, if I were him, I would go to school first. If he is to play professional ball, the teams will still be there in three or four years."

Thankful for his candor, Mr. James nodded his head in agreement. The four talked for a few more minutes about summer and the upcoming year.

Several hours later, sticky from the humidity, Julio laid on his bed and thought about Alexa.

26

Late June

Mike Williams

When we could, we liked to spend our summer evenings at Lake Herrin, which was up the road about thirty minutes from Franklin. Throughout the summer, small bonfires dotted the beach. Even in the winter, we found the time to drive up and relax on the beach under the stars. The only thing we lacked were crashing waves.

Nicole and Alexa approached the beach with their towels in hand.

Zach smiled as he noticed them walk our way. "Hey ladies, do you want a beer or a soda?"

Nicole and Alexa looked at each and smiled. Nicole replied, "I'm fine," followed by Alexa who responded like Nicole.

Ronald dug two beers out of the cooler. He looked at Nicole. "Com' on girl, have one."

Nicole shyly looked at Alexa. Neither of the girls were big drinkers, but they never turned down at least one drink if you persisted, which is why Ronald offered them a drink the second time.

"Okay, I guess it won't hurt to have one," Nicole said enthusiastically.

She looked at Alexa. "Com' on, have one. Live a little.

Alexa smiled. "Okay, why not?" she responded gleefully.

The police did not come to the area often throughout the week, so we were not too concerned about them. There were also enough college students on the small beach. Personally, I think the police in the area had other things to worry about.

As the night went on, we laid on the beach with our feet in the cool sand. It was more than relaxing. Alexa looked up towards the night sky several times. She must have been admiring the stars, because I know I was.

"So how's Dirk?" Zach asked jokingly.

"Dirk? You mean Julio, you big goon?"

"Oh yeah, him," he said with a smile. "You know, Alexa. I have to admit, I couldn't stand him at first, but the dude can flat out play."

"And?" She asked with a smile.

"And, what?" He asked.

"Is that all?" She asked him, pressing for more. "Come on, you have to admit you were a prick to him from the get go for no other reason than he was black."

Zach paused. "Yeah, you're right."

Alexa always had a way with words.

Nicole quietly sipped her drink as the playful exchange between Alexa and Zach played out. The lake breeze blew Nicole's hair off her shoulders which caught my attention. For some reason, I never asked Nicole out. Like Alexa, I figured she saw me as a friend and not much more.

After a while, Alexa and Nicole stretched out on their towels and looked up towards the vast night sky. "Man, look at those stars Nicole."

"Yeah, I know. They're beautiful," responded Nicole after taking a sip of her beer.

Alexa looked at Nicole. "Nicole," she said, "I'm going to go to school somewhere in California."

Nicole didn't say anything. She reached for Alexa's left hand with her right hand. The corners of her eyes began to tear up. Alexa squeezed Nicole's hand tighter because she heard Nicole sniff.

"Alexa...I haven't always been the most supportive friend this year. I'm glad you met Julio. He's good to you. You need him." Nicole fought every urge to start crying.

Alexa squeezed Nicole's hand tighter. "Thanks, that

213

means a lot. I'll need your support this year."

Nicole smiled.

"Forgive me for being such a bitch this past year."

Alexa, nearly in tears, turned her head in the sand to the left. "Sweetie, you're my friend. You don't need to apologize!"

Nicole smiled. "I can't believe I'm saying this, but I have a crush on Jeremy. He's a good looking guy."

Alexa looked at Nicole again. A cool silhouette formed around Nicole because of the bonfires. "Well, maybe we can go out as a group again."

Nicole looked at Alexa. "Yeah, I'd like that."

As the evening dragged on, Nicole and Alexa became more and more tired. The midday heat certainly didn't help. It had been over three hours since they had arrived.

Alexa looked at Nicole. "Let's get out here."

"Sounds...sounds good," replied Nicole as she emptied her soda can she had started once she finished her beer.

The rest of us remained on the beach when Nicole and Alexa headed back towards their car. The last thing any of us wanted to do was make the drive home. Granted, in the grand scheme of things, it wasn't a very long drive, but it was hilly and the threat of deer was always there.

Alexa sat in the passenger's seat and smiled as Nicole made her way through the hilly southern Illinois forest. "Nicole, I want to thank you for being my friend. I love you."

Before Nicole had a chance to respond, her eyes widened and a frantic look came across her face.

BANG! THUMP! BANG!

A deer rolled up and over her car which shattered numerous windows and crumpled the left side of the car. The car hit a ditch, flipped in the air, and landed upside down. The wheels spun and smoke billowed from the engine. Both girls sat in their seats upside down. They were held in place by their seat belts. On the side of the road laid two dead deer.

Alexa momentarily felt the world spin. She took a deep breath and shook her head. Her body shook from the adrenaline which flowed through her veins.

"Hey Nicole, are you okay?"

No answer.

"Nicole?"

No answer again.

Alexa, perplexed, looked to her left and screamed. Nicole was motionless. Blood dripped from her mouth. Frantic, Alexa shook her several times.

Hysterically, Alexa did all she could to unfasten her seatbelt, but her hands wouldn't stop shaking. She tried to move her legs but they were pinned in. She was trapped. Frustrated and scared, she muttered to herself.

Alexa looked at Nicole again. She still hadn't moved and blood continued to drip from her mouth.

"No, no, no, please wake up!" Alexa yelled.

Zach's phone buzzed. "No! No! No! Get your things dude!"

I confusingly looked at him. "Why? What's the hurry?"

"Alexa and Nicole have been in an accident up the road!"

We quickly gathered our things and ran towards my car. Thankfully, we had not had a drink since we got to the beach. Several minutes later we arrived at the scene.

The police and ambulance had already arrived.

The paramedics ran up to Alexa's door and smashed her window in. Caught off guard, she started to scream at the paramedics. While she screamed at Nicole to wake up, Alexa felt a pull on her right side.

The police started to smash the window and tried to open Nicole's door. Alexa heard voices from all sides, but it was too much to take in. Her senses were overwhelmed. It seemed the paramedics were talking in gibberish. The police did all they could to open the door on Nicole's side. Loud thuds and cracks startled Alexa at times.

An officer tugged on Alexa. "Are you alright?"

No answer.

He scanned Alexa for potential injuries with his flashlight. His flashlight stopped at her legs.

"Are you hurt anywhere?" the paramedic asked.

Alexa began to hyperventilate. Tears poured down her face as she looked at the officer.

"My friend, damnit! Get my friend!" she yelled.

The officer flashed his light to the driver's side. Nicole wasn't moving.

"Can you please get my friend?! Please!"

He worked to unfasten her seatbelt. "Shh... shh... you're going to be alright."

As he worked to remove her, she looked at the paramedic. "My legs, I can't move my legs!"

The next thing Alexa knew, she was being pulled from the car. She cried hysterically as her friend sat motionless. Tears streamed down her face as she yelled for Nicole.

She looked down. "My legs..."

Finally, the medics pulled her from the wreckage and

quickly put her on a stretcher. Over and over again she kept yelling, "My legs! I can't move my legs!" and "Nicole! Please get Nicole!"

Zach and I stood in shock as they helped Alexa. I wanted to help, but I didn't know what to do. I couldn't get over how mangled the car was. Scattered across the road were two huge ass deer. Nicole didn't have a chance.

I looked at Zach. "Let's get to the hospital...call your parents."

For such a tough guy, Zach was sure torn up. But then again, tough guys can cry too. "This sucks. This really sucks," he muttered.

Julio laid on his bed and began to slowly drift asleep. Both he and Jeremy were up later than normal because the Cardinals were on tv. The house phone rang. Julio looked at his clock and noticed it was one in the morning.

A few seconds later, Julio heard a knock on the door. Before a response was made, Mr. James walked in and looked at Julio with a frantic look on his face. "Get dressed!"

Julio didn't fully comprehend the situation. Instead, he continue to lay on his bed.

"That was Alexa's mom on the phone. There has been an accident. Alexa is in the hospital. She was in an accident with Nicole."

"Is Alexa hurt?" Julio asked frantically.

There was a pause. "Alexa is hurt. But Julio... the car hit two deer and flipped. Nicole didn't make it."

27

Late June

Mike Williams

It was nearly two in the morning when Julio and his dad approached the entrance to the emergency room. Nurses and doctors rushed from one place to another. Off to the side was Alexa's mom and dad. Zach and I, along with a few others, sat on the opposite side of the room. We were all at the lake when the accident occurred.

Julio stood in the middle of the waiting room, confused. As soon as Mrs. Sherman noticed Julio, she stood up and walked over to him. Julio reached out and hugged Mrs. Sherman and whispered, "Everything will be alright," as he fought off tears.

She mustered up a quivering smile as she wiped away her tears. She pulled Julio tighter. "I'm so glad you are here, darling. She's going to need you."

Mrs. Sherman noticed Julio's dad was standing by himself off to the side. She walked up to Mr. James and gave him a hug. By now, Mr. Sherman was next to his wife.

Mr. Sherman looked at Julio and then his dad. "Thanks so much for being here. Alexa loves you guys."

Julio hugged Mr. Sherman.

Zach and I moved up next to Alexa's parents. Julio paused for a moment, not quite sure what to expect. Then again, I don't really blame him. Julio reached out to shake Zach's hand. Like everyone else in the room, Zach had tears in his eyes. He looked at Julio's hand. Instead, he pulled Julio in and embraced him. Zach repeated multiple times, "Everything is going to be okay man. I am so sorry."

Like Zach, I gave Julio a hug. I noticed Mr. James off to the side. Tears were in my eyes, but that didn't stop me from walking over to Mr. James. "Hey sir, I'm Mike. I played third base for the team."

"Nice to meet you, Mike," Mr. James replied somberly.

Julio pulled Zach and I to the side. "So what happened?"

"They hit two deer and Nicole's car flipped after running off the road. I think the impact of the deer and the ground combined killed Nicole instantly. At least, that is what overheard. Nothing is official yet." Zach paused. "Dang, I still can't believe I saw them a few hours ago."

Julio was unresponsive.

Seconds later, Julio felt a thump on his shoulder. It was Zach. "You okay man? Be strong."

A half hour had passed. Zach and I did our best to keep Julio distracted. Honestly, of the three I think I was handling it the best, but then again, it wasn't until the next morning when I woke up truly crying. None of us knew what to say or how to say it. Alexa's health took our minds off of Nicole's death.

The doctor finally walked in the waiting room after what seemed to be eternity. It was obvious the years had taken its toll on him. Somberly, he looked throughout the room in search of Alexa's parents.

Fearful of the worst, Alexa's mom started to cry uncontrollably. "Ma'am, are you Alexa's mother?" he asked. "Can I talk to you and your husband for a moment?"

She sat in her seat and looked at her husband. Mrs. Sherman leaned into Mr. Sherman and clasped his side. He lovingly wrapped his arms around his beloved wife and squeezed. "Shh... Shh..." he whispered lovingly.

Her breaths became erratic. "Sir," she said while wiping away her tears, "if you don't mind, can you just tell us how she is?"

The doctor sat down on the bench next to Alexa's mom. He grasped Mrs. Sherman's hand. "Alexa is breathing fine and she's asleep right now. Her legs were badly damaged.

Her right leg was broken in numerous spots and her left leg was badly damaged as well. The bright side in all of this is she is alive and not paralyzed." He paused. "But she will need therapy."

We looked at each other. Zach sat back in his chair and took a deep breath. Relieved, Julio dropped his head. I smiled.

Mr. James leaned into Julio. "Everything is going to be alright. She's a fighter."

Julio looked at his dad. "It's just not right, dad."

"I know son, I know."

Across the room Mr. Sherman squeezed his wife tightly. "Everything is going to be alright."

Julio and his dad pulled into the driveway. A light was on in the kitchen. Julio walked by his mom with his head down towards the hallway which led upstairs.

The next two days were somber ones. Julio tried to motivate himself, but his mind had a tendency to wander. He somehow found the energy to fill out the application to Stanford, but that was about it. As much as he wanted to see Alexa, visitors weren't allowed except for family.

The morning of Nicole's funeral, the house phone rang. Moments later, Julio's dad was at Julio's bedroom door. "Son" he said quietly, "that was Mrs. Sherman. Alexa has asked about you this morning."

There was no answer.

Mr. James walked into the room and sat down on the bed next to Julio.

"I hate that I can't see her!"

"How about this? We stop by the hospital after the funeral. If they let us see her great. If not, at least we tried."

Julio's face brightened. "Yeah, that works."

Once the funeral was over, Julio, Jeremy and their dad headed towards the hospital to see Alexa.

"Dad, can we stop at the grocery store for a moment?" Julio asked.

"Sure."

They pulled into the local store. Julio made his way to the flower section. He had never bought flowers for a girl before. Thankfully, his dad was next to him the whole time. Julio looked at the flowers for a minute.

Troubled, Julio looked at his dad. "I have no clue what to pick."

His dad smiled. "Well, how about those?" He pointed to the dozen red roses behind one of the boutiques. "Does she like stuffed animals?"

"I have no clue," Julio added confusingly.

Mr. James nudged Julio and smiled. "Get her those flowers and that little teddy bear."

After the decision of a lifetime was made, they made their way towards the hospital. Once they arrived at the hospital, they quickly walked towards the front desk.

"Excuse me, we are here to Alexa Sherman. Is she taking guests?" Their dad asked politely.

Julio stood nervously next to his dad.

The nurse typed on her keyboard. "She is taking guests, sir. Sign here."

Julio smiled.

Moments later, he nervously approached the door to her room. As he raised his hand to knock on the door, thoughts rushed through his head...*what if she's asleep, what if she doesn't want to see me.*

He batted away his fears and knocked quietly on the door.

From the other side of the door he heard a soft voice. "Come in."

Super nervous, Julio paused. He took a deep breath and opened the door enough to peek his head through. "Alexa? Hello?"

As soon as she saw Julio, she perked up in her bed and smiled. She threw her hands in the air. "Julio, how are you doing smarty farty?"

Julio walked over and sat on the side of the bed. "I brought you these."

Alexa reached for her prized gifts as tears filled up in her eyes. "Oh, you didn't. I love these!" she exclaimed.

She brought the teddy bear to her face. "Oh, this is so soft."

"You like them?"

Lost in her gifts, she didn't answer.

Julio reached for Alexa's right hand and squeezed it.

Alexa's lips quivered. "Nicole told me the night she died I was lucky to be with you and she thought you were good to me."

"Well, she was growing on me as well. I know she was just looking out for you from the start. Nicole was a good friend to you."

Julio took Alexa's hand and put it up to her heart. "Remember, your best friend will always be here looking out for you and standing up for you."

Tears streamed down her face. Alexa turned her head to the left and pressed her face against the pillow. Julio quietly rubbed her right hand.

After nearly an hour another knock sounded at the door. Mr. James peaked in. "Sorry to bother you two, but we need to go Julio. We'll be back but she needs her rest."

He hugged her one last time. Alexa's room was empty again.

28

Mid August

Mike Williams

Finally, it was time to start school again. In many ways, I was glad to get back into the groove of school. I'm not sure about everyone else, but I know I was. Throughout the months of July and August, Alexa's legs began to slowly heal. She and her mom also filled out several college applications. One, of course, was to Stanford, the school she hoped to attend more than any other.

As for Julio? Well, he talked to several scouts throughout the summer, but he wasn't able to keep his mind focused on baseball. His thoughts were on Alexa.

The last month and half was especially hard on Alexa. One morning in early August she woke up and was ready for a change. "Mom?" she asked. "Can we have a girls' day? I want to get my nails done and my hair cut off."

"Really? Why's that?"

"I don't know. I just feel I need to get out of this funk I'm in."

Mrs. Sherman smiled. "Sure, honey. Let's finish our coffee and we'll head out."

I couldn't believe it when she sent me and several others a selfie of herself. Her hair was cut to her shoulders. Needless to say, everyone in the group text was surprised.

Zach was contacted by several universities for baseball and football. Most notably was the University of Kentucky. I guess they wanted him for football, much to the surprise of many -- including me, since I didn't think he was big enough.

Julio was in his room when the house phone rang. Minutes later, Julio's mom was at his bedroom door with a smile on her face.

"That was Mrs. Sherman on the phone. Go on over to Alexa's if you have a few minutes."

Julio immediately noticed Alexa on the porch when he pulled into her driveway. Her wheelchair was next to the swing. She was in the swing and sipping on her cup of coffee. To his surprise, her mom was outside on the swing as well, which was not the norm. *I hope I didn't do anything wrong* he immediately thought.

He approached the porch. "Morning ladies."

Both Alexa and her mom waved. "Surprised seeing you here this morning," Alexa said with a smile.

"Yeah, I was told to come over."

"Oh really? That's strange." She looked at her mom and winked.

Julio walked over and kissed Alexa on the cheek.

Mrs. Sherman smiled. "So have you heard anything from Stanford, yet?"

Julio paused. "Well, not since I applied. I have talked to the coach and he has offered me a scholarship. A few pro teams have contacted me as well, but if I go to a college it will be Stanford, unless something better comes along."

Both Alexa and her mom looked at each other. Alexa giggled, which made Julio smile. Since Nicole's death, Alexa spent many afternoons crying.

Tears formed in Alexa's eyes and a pitiful smile crept across her face. "Would you have any problems if I went to Stanford as well?"

"No!" he said without hesitation.

"Well, I got accepted into Stanford yesterday!"

An outpouring of emotions came to the surface. "I wanted to tell Nicole so bad!" she exclaimed.

Silence fell onto the porch. Both Julio and Mrs. Sherman sat quietly as Alexa cried.

A few minutes passed. She wiped away her tears and let forth a smile. "I...I'm sorry. But hey! I'm a Cardinal now," she said raising her arms in the air.

Julio stood up, walked over to her and wrapped his arms around her. "I'm so proud of you."

Mrs. Sherman smiled. "Julio, do you want to stay for lunch?"

Julio grinned. "I would love to."

"Good, because I wouldn't take 'no' for an answer."

Alexa sat on the swing with her acceptance letter in her hands. She couldn't help but notice the blue skies. She smiled.

29

MId August

Mike Williams

Julio walked through the doors of Franklin High School for the first day of his senior year. He looked at Jeremy and smiled. "Well, here we go."

Jeremy, less enthused about the start of school, shook his head. "Yep."

"Well, have a good day," Julio said with a grin. "This is my senior year."

Jeremy looked at him with a blank response.

Julio walked towards his first period class and Jeremy searched for a few of his friends he had made near the end of the previous school year.

In the far corner of our first period class sat Zach and I. As soon as Julio walked in, we noticed him, but then again, he was kind of hard to miss. I mean, he was kind of a big guy. When he looked at us, we both acknowledged him.

"Hey Julio, get your butt over here," I declared.

Zach was leaning back in his chair, as if he didn't have a care in the world. I guess I was as well but I never pretended to be as cool as Zach not to mention I knew I couldn't get away with it even if I tried.

"I see you guys are excited about school." Julio jokingly said.

"Thank God this is our senior year. I'm ready to get out of here," Zach replied. "Damn, I hate school."

I looked at Zach. "I thought you were going to college?"

Before Zach had a chance to respond, I looked at Julio. "So dude, are you really going to Stanford?"

Julio grinned. "Yep, that's the plan."

"What's the scoop on Alexa? Is she going there too?" Zach asked curiously. I wanted to know as well but Zach asked him first.

Julio shrugged his shoulders. "Don't know. You need to ask her."

Zach smiled. "Dude, if anyone knows it would be you."

"So how's the football team going to be?" asked Julio in hopes of shifting the line of questions. I mean, why else would he be asking? I mean, we all knew the answer. *Uh, average.*

Later in the day I pulled Julio to the side. "So where the hell is Alexa today?"

"Oh, she's in rehab," Julio responded.

I paused. "So how's that coming?"

Julio nodded his head. "It's coming from what I can tell. Some days she's hard to read...you know?"

I smiled. "Yeah, women."

Once school was done, Julio quickly drove Jeremy home. He didn't say a word the whole time. I guess he was focused on other things, like Alexa. Julio came to a stop in their driveway and looked at Jeremy. Slightly confused, Jeremy looked at his brother.

"I'm heading to Alexa's," Julio said adamantly.

Jeremy looked at Julio. He was slightly irritated Julio couldn't drive the extra 10 feet. "See yah later."

Alexa sat quietly on the porch swing prior to Julio's arrival. "What's on your mind, sweetie?" her mom asked.

Alexa didn't respond.

Mrs. Sherman leaned forward. "Sweetie?"

Alexa looked at her mom frustratingly.

Julio pulled into the driveway. Alexa wheeled her chair to the top of the porch stairs. Mrs. Sherman watched as Julio walked up to the porch.

Julio walked to the top of the porch and gave her a long hug.

"I missed you today," he whispered.

Alexa kissed him on the cheek. Choked up, she was

unable to respond.

Julio walked over to Mrs. Sherman and gave her a hug.

Julio plopped down on the porch swing. "So how are you lovely ladies today?" he asked with a smile.

"Well Julio, we're doing great," chimed Mrs. Sherman. She looked at Alexa with a nervous smile. "Alexa tell Julio the news you got today."

Aggravated at her mom, Alexa burst out, "Mom!"

Julio sat on the swing, not sure what to say or do. He looked at Alexa. "What's the news?"

Alexa, with a look of disdain, glance at her mom and then at Julio.

"The doctors told her she'd be out of the chair by October and using crutches. Isn't that great news?" Mrs. Sherman said with a smile as she clapped quietly.

"Why are you in tears?" he asked, confused.

Alexa looked at her mom with a blank stare. Her eyes were red from her crying.

"Can...Can you just shut up mom!?" Alexa said forcefully.

Mrs. Sherman looked at Alexa and then Julio. "I guess I need to go inside." She looked at Julio with her shoulders slumped. "I'm glad you came over."

Julio and Alexa sat quietly on the porch. Not quite sure what to say, Julio looked at Alexa.

She refused to make eye contact with him. "I..I think you should go," she said in a shaky voice.

He gave her a hug and stood up. Half way down the porch steps he paused. "You know, you're not the only one..." He paused.

"Only one what?!" she asked angrily.

"Oh nothing, it's doesn't matter."

"Doesn't matter, what? Hey Julio, what doesn't matter?"

He refused to turn around as he approached his car.

Julio got in his car and backed out. Alone on the porch sat Alexa. She put her head in her hands and cried uncontrollably. Images of her friend flashed in her head.

As Julio drove away, he angrily slammed his hand against the steering wheel. "What do you want from me?!" he yelled.

30

Late September

Mike Williams

Alexa was saddened she couldn't cheer her senior year. It depressed Alexa when she would go by the school trophy case. Nicole's cheer uniform was kept inside. If she did happen to go by the case, she would look away.

Unlike me, Julio was as diligent as ever when it came to his studies. I was just your average student. Every now and then a professional team contacted Julio or Coach Wilson. Every few days Zach was contacted as well. More so for football, but a few schools liked his talents at shortstop. Every once in a while a school would contact me as well. Heck, even a few major league teams were interested in me! Can you believe that? I couldn't!

The football team had started off on the right track with wins the first three games. Alexa hated the games because she could not be on the sidelines.

The Thursday before the Carbondale game, Julio stopped by Alexa's house. Her school books were open and her coffee cup sat on the porch.

"Hey babe." He walked up to her and kissed her on the

cheek. She edged her cheek towards him but she did not say a word.

Julio sat in the swing and leaned back.

"Alexa...Alexa? Hey?"

"What!" she yelled as she threw her books onto the ground. "You want to talk, okay let's talk, what do YOU want to talk about!"

Alexa leaned forward in her chair. "How about let's talk about the fact I'm in a freaken wheelchair, or how about my best friend died in front of me. Do any of those topics sound like fun freaken topics or do you have something else you want to talk about?" She was so angry her voice began to shake.

Julio sat in his seat motionless.

"Dude, I thought you wanted to talk. Hey, let's talk about how I can't cheer anymore, something I was hoping to do at Stanford. Nah, let's not talk about that. How about the fact everyone wants to be supportive, but I don't want your freaken help? Nothing you can say or do can bring back Nicole or take away the accident."

Julio looked away.

"I thought you wanted to talk! Uh...uh... say something! I just sit here and all you guys want to try and cheer me up. Did you ever ask me if I wanted to be cheered up? Hell no, of course not, because you guys know everything." She threw her hands in the air. "I'm just the stupid blonde in a wheelchair," she yelled.

Alexa started to hyperventilate.

He raised his head and looked at Alexa. "You know, Alexa? I never said thank you."

Confused, Alexa looked at Julio. "What the hell are you talking about?"

Julio leaned forward in the swing and looked at her and her tear filled eyes. "Well, I moved here, and I heard nothing but slams directed at me. I was told not to even to talk to you. I would go to games and would be told to move. Heck, even Nicole told me to stay away from you. I didn't feel welcomed AT ALL in this town." He paused momentarily.

"What does this have to do with anything?" she muttered.

Julio laughed sarcastically. "You don't get it, do you? You were there for me, even though you didn't know quite what to say or do, but just me seeing you made me happy. Well Alexa, I don't get it? Yeah, I don't understand what it's like to see a good friend die in front of me. Nope, you are damn right. I don't! But you know what? YOU were there for me and all I can do is be there for YOU. You don't like it? Sorry, but I'm not going anywhere, damnit. YOU had your chance to throw me to the side last year."

Her lips quaked. "Just help me get through this please. I feel alone and lost."

"Help you?" he repeated. "That's been my goal this whole time and I have no intentions on stopping now." He stood up and walked over to her. He leaned down and gave her a hug.

Alexa hugged Julio tight. "You better not leave me, you big jerk!"

31

Mid November

Mike Williams

The month of October came and went. Alexa had slowly improved and the need for a wheelchair had passed. To celebrate, Julio offered to take her out for pizza. The dark cloud which hovered over her started to subside. Prior to her date with Julio, she made sure her makeup was on just right. Once she approved her makeup, she thumbed through her closet in search of the right outfit. She finally located an outfit that would go with her crutches.

As the two made their way to Carbondale, Alexa couldn't stop beaming she was so happy.

Julio glanced at Alexa. "What are you smiling about?"

She giggled. "Oh...nothing. I'm just happy."

Julio reached over and gently grabbed her hand.

They finally reached their favorite pizza place. By now the sun had set and there was a slight chill in the air.

The server sat them in a booth away from the door.

Julio grinned at Alexa.

"What?" she asked curiously.

"You look amazing!"

She smiled. "You like? Well I know how much you like red and this sweater dress is one of my favorites."

"Hey, what's that cologne? Mmm, whatever it is, hold me back." she said with a flirty smirk.

They sat quietly in the booth across from each other while they waited for their pizza order to arrive.

He continued to grin at her.

"What?" She asked.

"Man I love those big blue eyes of yours."

She smiled at him proudly. "Thanks."

After a few minutes of silence Alexa chirped, "so have you heard any more from Stanford?"

"Nah, I haven't heard anything lately. I know you are worried about me going pro as opposed to Stanford. Let me say it right here and you can record it."

Alexa lit up like a firefly. "Oh I can record this, what am I recording?" She giggled as she fumbled for her phone.

She motioned for him to wait. "Wait...wait don't say anything yet."

She finally located her phone and turned it towards Julio. She pressed record. "Okay cowboy."

Now embarrassed, Julio did not know what to say. Alexa of course was happy to oblige. "You said you were not going to go pro and you said I could record it, which I am doing right now. So come on, speak up."

She motioned with her hands to speak up. She grinned devilishly in Julio's direction.

"You so took me the wrong way. I said I am not going pro unless there is a great offer," Julio said with a smile.

Alexa moved her phone to the side but continued to record him. "Ahhh I see how you are, get a big enough paycheck and you forget about little ole me huh," she said with a smile.

Julio looked at her and then the phone. "Okay give me a pen."

While recording him, she reached for a pen and pushed it towards Julio.

He grabbed the pen and quickly wrote a note on a napkin. Alexa noseley peered around her phone.

Julio looked up and smiled. "Is that thing still recording?"

"Oh, you know it is smarty farty," Alexa said happily. "What did you write mister?"

He grabbed the sides of the napkin with his two hands and held it up for the camera. Alexa peaked around the camera to get a better view of what she was looking at. She read the napkin to herself.

I won't go pro unless a California team drafts me

Saturday November 10, 2012

Alexa's jaw dropped. She immediately stopped recording. "What if St. Louis drafts you? Both you and I know they want you."

"Yeah I'd love to play for them, but I can always be drafted after going to college."

She struggled to stand up. Once up, she worked her way to his side of the table with the aid of her crutches. Julio, unsure if he said something wrong, sat in the booth confused and kind of worried. She devilishly looked at Julio as she threw her crutches to the floor. As if on que, all of the other customers looked in their direction because of the loud noise.

She leaned in, closed her eyes, and kissed Julio on his lips. As their lips met, Alexa could feel Julio run his hands through her hair and she loved it.

A number of customers continued to watch the show with enjoyment as Alexa and Julio kissed. I could only imagine what it looked like. I bet it was quite the show.

One yelled "that a boy" while a few others clapped with enthusiasm.

Alexa pulled away from his lips. "Let's get out of here," she said as she motioned towards the door with her head.

Julio motioned the server for the check, who was happy to oblige the two teens. As they made their way out the door, a number of college students turned and applauded them quietly.

As they passed by the last booth, they heard a voice quietly say, "dude, you'll be a fool if you let her go."

Julio pulled up to Alexa's house and stopped the car. He turned off the ignition and worked his way out of the car. He walked to the other side of the car to help Alexa. After she positioned herself with her crutches she blew him a kiss.

They made their way to the front porch. Both of them shivered in the cool November air. Alexa looked at Julio. There was just enough light to see him. "You aren't going home yet, are yah?" she asked with her patent pouty voice.

Julio put his right hand on the middle of her back for support as she worked her way up the steps. "Nah, I can stay here for a little bit."

They made their way to the swing and sat down. She leaned against him as she put her legs up on the porch swing. Alexa rested her head on Julio's lap.

He stroked her hair which totally put her at ease. It had been forever since someone had run their hands through her hair and she loved it.

"Just think, in a year we will be at Stanford," Julio said with a smile.

Alexa opened her eyes and looked at Julio. "I love to listen to the wind chimes. They are so relaxing."

With only a porch light on to see by, Julio looked down at Alexa and continued to smile as he stroked her hair.

Totally relaxed, Alexa closed her eyes.

Alexa's eyes popped open. "Do you hear that?"

"Here what?" he asked curiously.

"Shh... shh..." she immediately replied. "Those are sirens."

"Yeah, they are probably nothing." Julio responded.

Alexa looked at Julio. "Yeah, you are probably right."

Thirty minutes later, Alexa's house phone rang. Neither Alexa nor Julio thought much about the phone. They were in their own world.

Alexa's mom swung the door open. "Kids, that was Mike... Zach was in an accident out on Route Three."

32

Mid November

Mike Williams

I was in bed when Ronald called me. He had passed Zach after the accident. He called me in a panic. As you can imagine, when Alexa received the news about Zach's accident, she quickly wanted to leave for the hospital.

Her mom spoke up sternly. "Hun, you are NOT going anywhere tonight."

"What?!" Alexa exclaimed.

"No! You are in no condition to go. You can call Mike back and see what the situation is but you and Julio are going to stay put."

As she fumbled for her phone it buzzed from an incoming text.

I guess I timed my text perfectly.

Zach is okay, just a broken arm. Could've been much worse.

Alexa looked at Julio. "Thank God," she muttered.

Julio sat back in his seat. "Yeah, that would've sucked." He looked at his watch. "Well I need to run. It's getting late."

Alexa rolled her bottom lip. "Okay," she said sadly.

"Thanks again. I had a nice night."

The following Monday Julio walked into American Government class and immediately looked for Zach.

As soon as I saw Julio I acknowledged him with a nod. Julio acknowledged me back and walked towards the back part of the room. Those seats were claimed by us since the beginning of the year.

Julio sat and turned towards Zach and I.

I looked at Zach, then Julio. "Yeah, his car slammed into a ditch while dodging a deer. If he didn't have on his seatbelt, he would've hit the windshield."

Julio looked at Zach. "So how long will you have that cast on?"

Zach smiled. "Don't worry, you'll have to put up with me on the ball field. This cast should be off by late December."

Julio smiled. "Good, because it wouldn't be the same without your sorry butt out there. Right, Mike?"

"Hey don't get me involved in this," I replied jokingly.

Zach jumped in. "Yeah well both of you can go to hell."

I looked at Zach. "Why are you including me?!"

"Because I can," Zach quickly replied with a grin.

The class bell eventually rang which forced us to end

our verbal sparring. Well... for the time being anyways.

Monday, Tuesday, and Wednesday were all very normal days. Thursday was as well, until Julio was called out of class by his coach. Julio made his way to Coach Wilson's room. The lucky idiot. He was able to get out of class at the end of the day. What a nice surprise.

As soon as Coach Wilson noticed Julio he smiled. "Come with me."

Both Coach and Julio walked down to Coach Wilson's office without any words spoken between the two. Julio assumed it was another simple meeting with another college coach. When they approached the office door, Coach stepped to the side. "Go on in bud," he said with a grin.

Julio entered the room. In the corner of the office sat an older man with khakis and a brown and orange shirt. On the shirt, a capital *S* and *F* were printed above his heart.

Julio paused at the door momentarily. Once the shock wore off, he continued into the office and acknowledged the older man. Coach followed Julio into the office.

"Sit down, Julio."

Coach Wilson walked to the back of his desk and sat down. "Julio, this is Mike Dripps. He works for the San

Francisco Giants."

Julio stood up to shake Mr. Dripps' hand. After they shook hands, Julio sat back in his chair and nervously looked at his coach.

Finally, after a moment of silence, Mr. Dripps looked up from his notes. "Word has it you're leaning pretty heavily towards Stanford, son. Is that so?"

"Yes sir. That's true."

Mr. Dripps was intrigued. "What, may I ask, is the attraction to Stanford as opposed to going pro? If you don't mind me asking."

Julio leaned forward in his chair. "Well sir, I love the campus, what the school has to offer, and my girlfriend is also going there."

Coach Wilson looked at Mr. Dripps for his reaction.

"So... going pro is totally out of the question?" asked Mr. Dripps.

"Actually sir, if I was to be drafted by a California team, I would definitely think about it."

Mr. Dripps showed a hint of a smile. "Well... do you know why I'm here?"

Before Julio had a chance to answer, Mr. Dripps held up his cell phone and turned it towards Julio.

"I want you to watch this," he said with a plastered smile on his face.

Embarrassed, Julio put his face in his hands. "I'm going to kill her."

Coach Wilson covered his mouth and did everything possible to hide his laughter.

The video finally came to the end. Mr. Dripps leaned back in his chair. "Is this true?"

Julio was speechless.

"Well, we know St. Louis wants you, but if they catch wind of this they may not draft you. We follow them in the draft. So again, is this true? We'd love to draft you, if you're interested." Mr. Dripps paused as he shifted in his seat. "You'll be hearing more from us this spring. Think about it."

"Umm...Mr. Dripps, how did you get this video?" Julio had to ask.

Mr. Dripps looked at coach and then Julio. "The office received an email earlier in the week by a young woman that goes by the name of Alexa Sherman. Do you know her?"

Before Julio could answer, Mr. Dripps cut him off. "Again, we will be in contact. All I have to say is, don't lose that girl."

Mr. Dripps stood up and reached towards Julio with his hand. "I hope you become a Giant, son. We'll be talking."

33

Mid January

Mike Williams

By January Alexa didn't have to rely on her crutches to move, even though she still had a slight limp. Zach's cast had also been removed. Julio still planned to attend Stanford after graduation. As for me, I just kept doing my thing. I started to date a girl named Stephanie, but outside of that, I was ready for baseball to start.

The basketball team had another average season, which is probably why everyone was ready for baseball to start. Because of the cold temperatures, Julio and his brother threw in the gym every few days. Heck, even Kory Wilson and Kyle Whitten joined Julio and Jeremy. Yep, I was impressed.

It was mid-January when Julio was called out of P.E., which was fine with him. As soon as he walked into the coach's office he noticed a familiar face from the fall. It was Mike Dripps of the San Francisco Giants.

Mr. Dripps greeted Julio with a smile. To Julio's surprise, there was also another man next to Mr. Dripps.

"Hey Julio, good to see you. This is Sam Smith. He also

works for the Giants," which was evident because he had on a similar polo shirt as Mr. Dripps.

"Afternoon sir," Julio said with a smile.

The meeting lasted for nearly an hour. Both Mr. Smith and Mr. Dripps talked to Julio about the drafting process, the positives of choosing college over professional ball, and vice versa. They also talked about the various farm systems in the Giants organization. Of course, Coach Wilson asked a question or two from time to time.

As they began to finish up the meeting, Mike Dripps looked at his partner and then Julio. "Before we leave, we need to ask, how serious are you about going pro?"

Julio looked at Mr. Dripps nervously. "I... I'm wanting to play professionally more than anything, but I've made commitments. Depending on the situation, I will seriously think about it and put everything into my consideration, including my education, my commitments to Stanford, and even my girlfriend."

Julio stood up, shook their hands, smiled, thanked them for their time, and left the office.

After Julio left, Sam Smith looked at his partner and then Coach Wilson. "What's the deal with this girlfriend bit? Can we rely on him if we draft him or not? What do you think as his coach?"

Coach Wilson looked towards the door and then at the two men sitting in front of him. "Well sir, when he moved here, Alexa was the only one who gave him the time of day. Let's just say this town is not the most open to minorities. So it stands to reason he's committed to her. Not to mention she's an awesome person. So if you're asking me if you should take a chance on him, well, he's a great player. The best I've ever coached. The rest I'll leave up to you." Coach Wilson smiled as he leaned back in his chair.

While the meeting took place, school had ended and the building had emptied. Julio made his way towards his car.

Jeremy stood impatiently at the car. "Let me guess, you were talking to a scout or a recruiter."

Julio smiled.

Jeremy continued. "Next time, let me know, will ya?"

"Are you freaken serious? I was called in at the last moment. You'll understand in a few years, so just shut up."

34

Mid March

Mike Williams

As baseball got closer, Alexa did all she could to monopolize her time with Julio. One evening, Alexa and Julio were on the porch swing enjoying the weather. Alexa sipped on her typical cup of coffee, while Julio worked on a mug of hot chocolate. If you ask me, I was definitely a hot cocoa kind of guy myself, especially if whip cream and sprinkles were found on top. Amazingly, the few times I was over at Alexa's house, she had those two items.

Alexa looked at Julio and smiled. Julio was deep in thought, so she poked him in the side.

Startled, Julio spilled his drink.

"Oops, I'm so sorry!" she bellowed in laughter.

Julio smiled.

She bit her lower lip and grinned. "What about we go out Friday night?" She stood up. "I mean, I can walk now without a limp and baseball is nearly here…"

He cut her off. "How about Jeremy and his little girl friend come out as well? They can't drive and this would be fun to watch."

"It's not the same, but it sounds fun just the same. There is a cool place down in Cairo we can go to for pizza."

Julio looked at Alexa. "Are you sure you're good with it?"

Alexa smiled. "Yes, it would be fun."

Julio quickly texted Jeremy.

Call Jamie and remind her you'll be with us

Jamie, who was from Carbondale originally, moved with her parents to Franklin while in junior high. She was a year younger than Jeremy. She was also about the same height as Alexa at 5'5". She had long brownish blonde hair that flowed to the middle of her back, blue eyes, and a small figure.

Friday afternoon came quickly. Julio and Alexa walked through the student lot without a care in the world. The whole time they held hands and laughed as they walked. As they neared the car, they noticed an impatient Jeremy next to the car.

"You guys take forever," Jeremy said emphatically.

Amused, Julio looked at his brother. "Dude, this is the same as any other day."

Alexa smiled. She poked Jeremy in the side. "What? Are you a little nervous, dude?"

"Relax man. You need to act cool like me and the girls will eat it up," Julio said with a smirk on his face.

Alexa's jaw dropped. "What? You act cool? I had to ask you out! Please Jeremy, don't listen to him. Just be yourself tonight."

Julio looked at Alexa and then Jeremy. "That is the last thing you want to do, bro. You need to act tough. Girls love that."

Jeremy was ready to get home, so he did everything he could to zone them out. Julio and Alexa bantered back and forth over who asked whom out first. They must have forgotten Jeremy was in the car or they didn't care. Jeremy regretted the whole conversation. Not to mention Jeremy thought they sounded like an old married couple.

They dropped Alexa off at her house and agreed they would pick her up before they would pick up Jamie. As Jeremy got ready, he nervously paced back and forth. This was his first true date, and even though his brother and Alexa would be along, he was still nervous.

"What do you think? Jeans and shirt work?"

Julio smiled. "Dude, you are worse than a girl."

They pulled into Alexa's driveway. Alexa, of course, was out on her porch waiting for them. Her mom sat with her and kept her company. As soon as Alexa saw Julio's car, she stood up and ran down the porch steps.

Julio couldn't believe his eyes.

He nudged his brother. "Hey, look! She's wearing heels again! Doesn't she look awesome?"

"Girl, you look amazing in those boots and jeans."

"I know right. I couldn't wait to wear these." she added with a flirty smile. "You like my sweater? It's red. I wore it for you."

"I love it." Julio added.

She turned towards Jeremy, who had moved to the back seat, and winked. "Dude, you need to relax!"

A few minutes passed before they pulled into Jamie's driveway. Before Jeremy had a chance to get out of the car, Jamie was out of the front door. She quickly walked towards the car.

Jeremy frantically got out of the car to greet her.

Alexa looked at Julio. "Huh, that's strange."

"What's strange?"

"I don't see her parents anywhere."

Jamie got in the back seat next to Jeremy. Alexa turned around and smiled. "So why in the world would you want to go out with a loser like this?" she asked playfully.

Julio chimed in. "Yeah, of all the losers in the school, you picked my brother."

Alexa continued to smile. "By the way I'm Alexa and this big lunk is Julio."

Since she was slightly overwhelmed all Jamie could do was smile. She wasn't much of a talker either.

As they made their way towards Cairo, Alexa and Jamie talked. Julio just listened. Poor ole Jeremy sat nervously beside Jamie.

They finally reached their destination. Both Julio and Alexa had heard good things about **Franco's Pizza** which is why they wanted to go there, as opposed to their normal spot in Carbondale. As they walked in, Julio could feel something wasn't quite right about the place. He just could not put a finger on what it was. Alexa lead the way to their booth next to a window.

The server, who was in her mid 30s, came over and sheepishly smiled at Alexa. "Can I help you?"

Alexa smiled awkwardly. "Yeah, we'd love to order our drinks if that's possible."

The server looked at Alexa and Jamie followed by quick glances at Julio and Jeremy.

After Alexa and Jamie requested their drinks, Alexa

stood up. "I need to go to the bathroom, you want to come?" She asked Jamie.

The server approached the table seconds after the girls left. She didn't have a smile on her face, but instead she wore a frown. She stopped in front of Julio and looked at him.

Julio looked at her, confused.

"Don't you have any colored girls you could be dating?" She asked sternly.

Julio looked at her. "Colored girls? What decade are you in, lady?"

Alexa looked at the server as she approached the table. "Is there a problem, miss? I know I'd like to have my drink, as would the others at this table."

"No, we're just leaving." Julio said adamantly. "We don't need to eat here."

Alexa, Jeremy, and Julio began to walk out the door when they noticed Jamie alone at the table, visibly confused. Alexa walked back towards Jamie. "C' mon Jamie! We're not eating here! I will explain outside."

Confused, Jamie put her head down and walked outside with the rest of the group.

After they worked their way into the car, Alexa looked

at Jamie. "Sweetie," she said in a serious tone, "I want you to understand not everyone around here is fine with white girls going out with black guys. That server was racist, which is why we left. If you can't handle that then save Jeremy the agony, okay? If you can handle it and have a tough skin, then Jeremy will be worth it. Trust me." Alexa looked at Julio and smiled as she reached for his hand.

"Okay," she muttered to Alexa as she put her head on Jeremy's shoulder.

Alexa tapped the top of Julio's hand. "Hey! You antagonizer! There's a cool seafood place down the road." She looked back at Jamie who was obviously upset. "Is seafood okay?"

Jamie nodded.

35

Late March

Mike Williams

The first day of tryouts had finally arrived. We actually scoffed at the notion of it being tryouts, since almost everyone who "tried out" made the team. For some reason, we had a few more come out than in years past. Part of it must have had to do with our success the previous year.

The day of dragged on for many of us. Nothing is more painful than sitting in a boring class and waiting for the final bell to ring.

From across the room, Alexa giggled as she watched us squirm in agony as the day crept to a close. When the bell finally rang, we booked it to the locker room to change.

As the team stretched, Coach Wilson and Jacobs looked at the team in front of them. Coach Wilson couldn't stop smiling. I think he was as excited as we were the season had finally started.

As we stretched, one of the freshmen began to talk. Julio looked at him sternly. "Hey freshman, shut up."

Zach looked me and laughed. "Dumb freshmen," he whispered.

Between throwing, hitting in the cage, fielding balls off the gym floor, and throwing some more, the first week went by pretty fast. After a quick week, Zach and I stayed after practice to talk to Coach.

We approached the office door. Zach paused then proceeded to knock on the door.

There was a silence on the opposite side of the door.

"Coach, can we come in?" Zach asked nervously as he opened the door.

Coach smiled. "Come in. What's up?"

We slowly entered the office and sat down.

"Coach," Zach said as he looked at Coach Wilson, "I know I can speak for Mike and a few others. I know the topic of captain will come up eventually."

Zach paused.

"Well... we've been talking... and... well... we think it would only be right to have Julio named as one of the captains."

Coach Wilson leaned back in his chair and covered his face. As I look back, I think it was to hide a smile. He looked at Coach Jacobs first, then us. "Let me talk it over with Coach and I'll take your request into consideration. May I ask why?" He looked at me.

Of course I was caught off guard. "Um...um well, um sir, we feel he has proven himself as a player and a leader. He may not be vocal, but... um... he sure busts his butt every day."

Coach Wilson tapped his hands on the desk in a quick *rap puh pat pat* rhythm. "Sounds good guys. I appreciate you coming in. Now go home and have a good weekend." Coach stood up and reached across his desk to shake our hands.

We turned around and began to walk outside when I stopped. "Do you think we can make it to state this year?"

Coach Wilson smiled. "Son, this may be the best team that has ever played here at Franklin, but it's up to you guys to prove it. Can you do that?"

I smiled. "Yes sir. We'll sure try. Thanks for your time."

"Yea, thanks again, Coach," Zach added.

Once the office was emptied, the two coaches looked at each other. "Well son of a gun," Coach Wilson said with a surprised grin on his face.

Coach Jacobs looked at the door. "I DID NOT see that coming."

Coach Wilson nodded his head. "Let's get the heck out of here before anything else goofy happens."

36

Early April

Mike Williams

With baseball underway, the spring wasn't as warm as I would have liked it to have been. Julio would remind us of how much worse it could've been if we were up in northern Illinois. From time to time, Julio would glance at the Palo Alto temperatures and compare them to our dreadful temps.

Finally, our first game was just a day away. The team had been hitting off of the T for much of practice. If you were wondering, a T consisted of a waist high rubber tube that sat on home plate. Coach liked to use the T, so we would focus on our hitting mechanics.

The lights to the field were turned on because the sun began to creep below the horizon. Zach stepped in and ripped ten balls into left and right center.

After his last ball, Zach looked at Julio and smiled. "Top that big man."

Julio laughed.

He stepped up to home plate and scanned the field. Julio ripped eight in row into the outfield.

As the balls sailed into the outfield, the guys screamed and yelled with enthusiasm.

Zach stood 10 feet from Julio as he hit the ball. Every time Julio hit the ball, Zach made a snide comment. "Is that all you got? That's nothing. Come on, you wimp! Geeze, your girlfriend could hit harder than that."

Julio did his best to ignore him, but found it very difficult. Julio couldn't help but smile a few times after he hit the ball.

After his eighth swing, Julio stepped out of the box and smiled devilishly at Zach.

Zach grinned back. "C'mon you sissy! Hit the ball."

Julio planted his feet, paused, and swung. He swung so hard a grunt could be heard from right field where I was standing.

The ball flew off the tee with lightning speed towards me. At first I began to make an attempt on the ball, but then I realized it was over my head, so I stopped to watch it.

The ball hit the scoreboard with a loud THUMP! Instead of dropping to the ground like the hundreds of times prior, the ball remained lodged in the scoreboard. I stood in front of the scoreboard in disbelief. I waited for it to drop, but it never did!

I turned towards the infield. "Holy Crap! It's freaken stuck!"

The Coaches looked at each other in amazement.

Zach looked at the scoreboard and then Julio. "Holy crap! What did you have for breakfast?!"

Julio looked at his bat, the scoreboard, and then his coaches. "Coach, I'd like to end on that one, if you don't mind."

In disbelief, Coach looked at Julio. "Hell, I would too."

Enthusiastically, the rest of the team ran in from all parts of the field.

As for me, well, I had to turn and look at the scoreboard one more time. *Crap, that dude is a beast* I thought to myself.

It took the team a little longer to settle down, but once they did, Coach Wilson calmly pointed towards right field. "Guys, I'm not going to lie to you. This has been a tough year for you and me, but I have seen every one of you grow. I have one question for you." He paused as he looked at each of us seniors, starting with Zach. "Are you content with what we have accomplished or do you want more? Before you answer, think about this. What you do on the field and how you carry yourselves says a lot about you. Prove to your teammates, prove to me, and prove to this community you want more."

37

Early April

Mike Williams

Julio sat silently on the bench as he waited for the umpires to start the game. Many of the guys moved through the dugout like restless ants. Julio lifted his head and looked at two of his teammates.

"Hey freshmen, do you care about this game?" The two looked at him surprised. He paused to let them respond.

Zach chimed in. "If you're not ready to play baseball, get the hell out. We don't need you here."

Julio looked at Zach. "Freshmen." he scoured.

Zach walked up to Julio and hit him on the butt. "Let's kick some Doraville butt today."

Julio smiled.

The game did not quite start the way any of us hoped it would. The first two batters got weak hits to the right side of the field. After a sacrifice bunt and a flyout to center, Franklin was down by one. Julio finally worked his way out of the inning with a strikeout.

Considering the game was against Doraville, the bleachers did not fill up nearly as fast. Many chose to wait until the game had started because it was still quite cold outside.

Alexa sat in her normal spot up on the bleachers by the fence. The seat next to her that had previously been held by Nicole sat cold and empty.

Jamie hesitantly approached the bleachers. She noticed Alexa was by herself. "Can...can I sit here?"

Alexa smiled. "Come on, feel free. You must cheer though."

Doraville's lead didn't last long once our bats caught fire. We scored two to three runs in every inning. We eventually won the game 12 to 1. The season had begun!

38

Late April

Mike Williams

With each passing day, the flowers bloomed and the grass became greener. We rattled off twelve victories in a row. Many of the wins were off some bad teams, but in that run we did beat Carbondale. Julio and the rest of the pitching staff was unhittable and our offense was hitting the tar out of the ball. We must have averaged nearly ten runs a game.

Alexa and Jamie attended every game together. Kyle's girlfriend, Brandy, who was a sophomore like Kyle, sat with them for many of the home games. My girlfriend, Stephanie, came to most of the games as well, but she wasn't a big baseball fan... or so she said.

Jamie's personality reminded Alexa a lot of Nicole. I didn't see it, but Alexa thought the two were very similar.

Almost every day Coach Wilson received calls from colleges or professional scouts. Because of our success, word had gotten out about Julio, Zach, Jeremy, and even Kyle and I.

After we beat up on Walton in five innings, Alexa drove

Jamie back to her house. Jamie had grown to like coffee as much as her older friend, who had seemly taken her under her wing. The girls shivered in the cool air as they waited for Julio and Jeremy.

Jamie looked towards the street. "How did you make it through this past year?"

Alexa moved her hair to her side and smiled. "What do you mean?"

Jamie continued to look towards the street. "Well, you were dating someone who was not accepted here and then your friend died. Then, to top it off, you were in the accident and got injured in the process."

Alexa looked at Jamie. "Well, sometimes other people have issues greater than yours, which keeps you in check."

At that moment, Julio's car pulled into the driveway.

Jamie laid her head against the post, pondering Alexa's words of wisdom.

Julio and Jeremy reached the porch. "What are you two fine women talking about tonight?" Julio asked confidently.

"Us *fine* women are going prom dress shopping tomorrow," Alexa said with her pretend attitude.

Julio smiled on the outside, but on the inside his stomach turned in knots.

39

Mid May

Mike Williams

The regional tournament quickly approached. Both Vienna and Cartersville wound up not being much of a match for us. The games were close, but there was never a doubt who was going to win.

In between games, Julio found the time to make it to the local tuxedo store to get fitted.

"What are yah wearing?" he would ask Alexa repeatedly.

Alexa would just smile. "Something red...If I tell you more I'd have to shoot you and we don't want that...I can't tell you, it's bad luck," were the standard answers.

"Thanks for letting me take the day off, mom," Alexa said with a smile.

Mrs. Sherman looked at Alexa. "You're welcome. You had to get your nails done, right?"

Alexa grinned. "Ha, that's right."

I looked around the room during the last period of the day. I nudged Julio. "Dude, where are all the girls?"

Julio smiled. "I guess Alexa's getting her nails done."

I rolled my eyes. "Ugg, prom."

Julio pointed his finger at me. "I concur."

Once the bell rang, we walked down to the ball field. We didn't have any girls to slow us up for once either. Thankfully, practice ended early.

Once practice was over, Julio went home and ate dinner. Excited to see Alexa, he wolfed down his dinner and ran out the door. He pulled into Alexa's driveway. Of course, Alexa was in her normal spot on the porch. Imagine that!

To his surprise, I was there with Stephanie. As we settled into conversation, a light drizzle began to hit the ground.

"NO! Not rain!" Alexa bellowed.

Julio shrugged his shoulders as he looked at me. "Why? What's wrong? The field could use a little rain..."

Alexa interrupted him in mid-sentence. "No! No! Rain are YOU nuts! Uggg, YOU baseball players."

As the drizzle continued to fall, Julio and I shared with each other which teams were going after us.

As the conversation wore on, Stephanie interrupted us. "Alexa, how do you feel about Julio going somewhere far to play?"

Alexa shrugged her shoulders. "I'm not worried. I figure

if Julio and I are meant to be together, things will work out. Otherwise, I'm going to do what I'm going to do and I don't want to stop him either."

Stephanie huffed. She didn't like Alexa's answer.

Not long after Julio left, I decided it was time to go. As I stood up, Alexa smiled. "Mike," she said softly, "thanks for being you."

I looked at Alexa confused. "What do you mean?"

"Ah, you know. This past year hasn't always been easy for Julio or me. So, thanks."

"Girl, you don't need to thank me. You're a friend of mine. As for Julio, you know this place. All we needed was some time to get to know him. He's a great guy." I paused for a moment. "Wouldn't it be cool if we won the state title and both get drafted? I mean, we are a small town in the middle of nowhere. How often does that happen?"

"Dude, it's going to happen," Alexa responded confidently.

40

Mid May

Mike Williams

Prom day had finally arrived. It could not have come soon enough for Alexa. As excited as she was, she was nervous. Julio, on the other hand, felt ill.

Julio peered outside his window and smiled. The birds were chirping happily and the sun glistened on the wet grass. Julio turned from the window towards Jeremy. Smiling devilishly, Julio walked slowly across the room on his tiptoes as if he were the famous Cat Burglar.

He leaned over Jeremy's bed. He placed his hands on Jeremy's side. "Get up! Get up!" he yelled.

Startled, Jeremy kicked his legs into the air. "Arg!" He yelled.

Julio stepped back and smiled. Julio turned and made his way into this bathroom.

Jeremy shook his head. "I'm going to get him one of these days," he muttered.

Five minutes later, Julio walked out of the bathroom.

Jeremy wiped his tired eyes. "Dude, you know we have the day off, right?"

Julio laughed. "Oh, I know." He paused. "I just hate sleeping in."

"Well that doesn't mean I don't want to sleep in." Jeremy paused. "So are you excited about the prom?"

"Not really, but it's important to Alexa."

Needless to say, it was nice to have day off. As the afternoon wore on, Julio texted Alexa: *I'm **thinking of you** and **I can't wait for tonight***, which of course made her smile each time.

He was at the kitchen table when he noticed the time. "Shoot! I need to get ready." He ran upstairs and jumped in the shower all in a matter of seconds.

Even though he didn't know what Alexa's dress looked like, he knew it was red. Alexa told him to dress accordingly. Like every good young man, he knew it meant he needed to match Alexa. So he rented a black tuxedo with a red tie and vest. In all honesty, I had the same quandary with Stephanie.

Finally dressed, he called for his mom. She walked into his bedroom and stopped in her tracks.

Curious, Mr. James followed his wife upstairs.

Julio looked at his parents. "So how do I look?"

His mom smiled with pride. "Son, you look amazing! Alexa is one lucky girl."

Mr. James smiled proudly. "Yeah, you look great son."

Julio gathered his keys and wallet along with the corsage he had kept in the refrigerator.

Alexa nervously sat in her room. As if she was a princess locked in a castle, she ran to the window when she heard Julio's car pull into the driveway. She squealed with excitement as he walked towards the front door.

Alexa's mom opened the front door before Julio had a chance to knock. Like some bad spies, Julio's parents followed him from behind. Alexa's mom noticed them and smiled, followed by a wave.

"So you must be Julio's parents!" Mrs. Sherman said with a smile.

Alexa quickly looked at herself in the mirror. She smiled giddily.

Julio glanced behind and wondered if his parents were going to come inside the house. Out of the corner of his eye he noticed Alexa walk slowly down the stairs. Yeah, he was in love.

"Wow," Julio muttered with a smile. His mouth dropped as if the hinges on his jaw broke off. Alexa beamed with joy.

Mrs. James whispered to Mrs. Sherman. "I love those black heels.... and that red on them is so her."

Julio couldn't stop looking at her. "Wow Alexa. I love your hair."

Alexa smiled.

"Yeah, I love how it's wrapped over your left shoulder."

"Thanks!" She replied.

Mrs. Sherman and Mrs. James looked at each other. "That dress looks amazing on her. I love that cherry red color on your daughter."

Mr. Sherman playfully nudged Julio. "Mrs. Sherman, did you help pick that dress out? I don't like how it shows off her right leg.

Alexa looked at Julio. "Um, you don't look so bad yourself!"

Julio blushed. "Nah, I'm just trying to keep up."

Mr. James nudged Julio. Julio took the red corsage from his dad and put it on Alexa's wrist. Both Alexa's and Julio's parents snapped pictures with their phones.

The white limousine arrived soon after. He guided his date down the steps and towards the limo.

Franklin is a small town, so it did not take long for the

limousine to reach my house. Like Julio and Alexa, we experienced some of the same drama with the parents.

As soon as the limo pulled into my driveway, Alexa stretched across Julio and rolled down the window. She stuck her torso out the window and began to whistle at Stephanie and me as we walked out of the house.

Julio sat in the car seat and grinned nervously. The door swung open on the opposite side of Julio. Stephanie sat down across from Julio and I followed her into the car.

The limo pulled out of my driveway. The drive to Carbondale seemed much longer than normal. Probably because Stephanie and Alexa were more than wired. I mean, I was excited, but not nearly as excited as those two. Poor Julio. I think he was just trying to keep up.

We finally arrived at this cool 1920s hotel which was built across from the Southern Illinois campus. We walked inside the building and were immediately in awe with the chandeliers.

Alexa nudged Julio. "Look at those lights."

Julio smiled. Talking was fruitless because of the loud music.

Neither one had been to a prom, so they did not know what to think. In subtle amazement, Julio and Alexa knocked at balloons as the balloons floated by. Others felt compelled to pop the balloons.

We all danced throughout the evening, and when we weren't dancing, we watched everyone else. It was quite entertaining at times. As I said, conversation was fruitless because the music was so loud. Though he wasn't much of a dancer, Julio did his best. I should add, I'm not much of a dancer either and it was pretty evident.

As the time approached 11 o'clock, Alexa looked at Julio and motioned towards the floor with her head. Julio looked at me. "Well bro, I need to take my woman out for one more dance. You just going to sit there, are ya?"

I looked at Stephanie and motioned her to the floor. Stephanie gleefully jumped to her feet. Julio took Alexa's hand and guided her to a corner of the room where he held her tight. While her head rested against his chest, she could feel soft kisses on her head.

She looked up. "I wish this evening will never end."

He smiled. "Oh, I think the best is yet to come."

She smiled.

41

Late May

Mike Williams

After prom, we wound up winning four more games to finish 20-0 and first in the region. We entered the week with a two game bye since we were the number one seed. Our first game wasn't until Thursday evening against Carbondale, who had a disappointing year.

Coach Wilson pulled Julio and his brother to the side as they entered the school building the day of the game. "Julio, follow me."

Julio looked at his brother and motioned with his head for him to move on. He followed Coach Wilson to the coach's office and sat down.

"So? Are you ready to go tonight?" Without awaiting a response, Coach continued. "I hope we can get a good game out of Kyle tonight and then use you Saturday."

"Sounds good, Coach."

Many of us sat irritably in our seats while others tapped with their pencils onto their desks as the clock slowly moved towards the final seconds of the school day.

Game one was finally here. Kyle confidently took the

mound. The first few innings flew by uneventfully. We took the lead in the third inning with a single to center field.

In between the third and fourth innings, Alexa noticed Julio's parents. Alexa looked at Jamie. She stood up and straightened her pants. Jamie looked at her with confusion.

Alexa tugged on Jamie's shirt. "Come on girlfriend, you're coming with me."

Jamie followed her down the bleachers and behind the dugout. In the distance, Jamie noticed a set of parents in two lawn chairs.

"Come on Alexa, nooo," Jamie declared.

"Oh yes," Alexa said as she winked at Jamie.

Enthusiastically, Julio's mom stood up.

"It's so good to see you, Mrs. James!" Alexa said gleefully. "It's been a few weeks."

"Sweetie, you need to come by one evening for some dinner," Mrs. James said with a smile.

Mr. James worked to watch the game while he listened to his wife's conversation with Alexa.

"I saw you guys over here, so I wanted to introduce Jamie to you. I wasn't sure if you had met."

Mr. James stretched out his hand. "It's very nice to meet you. Jeremy thinks the world of you. I'm Frank and this is Pam. Feel welcome to come over anytime. Okay, hun?"

Shocked and nervous, Jamie's body churned inside. After a few long minutes, Alexa and Jamie walked back to their normal spot on the bleachers.

After a few minutes, Alexa looked at Jamie. "Are you okay?"

Jamie looked at Alexa with a tear in her eye. "Why did you do that?"

Alexa sighed. "I'm sorry. I didn't mean to make you feel uncomfortable."

Jamie looked away. "Yeah I know, just didn't know if they'd like me."

"Oh please, you're freaken adorable," Alexa said as she crinkled her nose and poked Jamie in the side.

Reassured, Jamie found a way to smile.

"Let's watch the game and cheer on our hunks," Alexa added playfully.

Alexa glanced up at the scoreboard. "Oh wow! They are up by six now. Geeze! Man we must have been oblivious!"

We eventually won two innings later. The next opponent was Vienna, who beat Cartersville in extra innings.

42

Late May

Mike Williams

The morning of the regional final, Julio awoke to his alarm. The room was still dark because the sun had not yet come up fully. The birds sang as if they had just found their voices. Across the room, Julio could hear his brother quietly snoring. *Jeremy had the right idea*, he thought to himself.

Julio's phone lit up from a received text. He rolled over to see who had text him. Of course, it was from Alexa. **Good luck tday, you will do great, luv you xoxo.**

He smiled. **Thnks, luv you too.**

A few streets away, Alexa kicked her legs up and down under her sheets as she giggled with happiness. He had never said *I love you* before. She put her phone down, paused, took a few deep breaths, and looked at her phone again.

Coach Wilson tried to sleep but couldn't, so he decided to show up early and work on the field. Apparently I wasn't normal, because I slept wonderfully. The players eventually arrived at the field, a few at a time, to hit in the cages. A little before 11 o'clock, the Vienna bus pulled into the parking lot next to the baseball field.

The fans filled in on both sides. Jamie sat on the bleachers next to Alexa. "Dang these fans are loud."

Alexa looked at Jamie and grinned. "Yep, it's Vienna! They're nothing but a bunch of hicks!"

Finally, it was game time. The sun was high in the sky. From time to time a puffy cloud floated by and hid us from the sun. Jeremy walked in from the pregame warmups. He shook his left hand several times in pain.

He looked at me, wincing.

"Is your brother throwing hard today?"

He held up his hand which was bright red. Yep, he was throwing hard alright. Point made.

The lead-off batter for Vienna stepped into the batter's box. Julio stepped into his motion.

Julio released the ball!

"Strike one!" the umpire declared. The championship game had begun.

Julio worked the batter to a full count against the Vienna batter. The game was in the sixth inning and we were up 2-1. Vienna had runners on second and third with two outs.

Julio stepped onto the rubber located on the mound

after he took a moment to compose himself. Jeremy squatted into his position behind home plate and glanced at the batter's feet. To his surprise, the batter was looking for an outside pitch.

Jeremy called for a fastball on the inner part of the plate. Julio called him off. Emphatically, Jeremy put the sign down again only to be called off by Julio a second time.

Irritated, Jeremy fell to his knees, threw off his mask, and turned towards the umpire. "Time out blue."

The umpire raised his arms in the air. "Time!"

Jeremy ran to the mound. Both of them put their gloves to their face so no one could read their lips.

"Dude, I want a fastball inside. He's looking outside off the plate. Don't throw that damn curve. He'll drive it," Jeremy said.

Julio nodded his head. "Sounds good. Get your sorry butt back there."

The batter's feet were in the same spot as before.

The pitch was delivered. The ball moved up and in on the batter. The batter swung and missed, which ended the inning and the threat.

The bottom of the sixth proved to be fruitless for our offense. The score remained 2-1 in our favor as we went into the seventh inning.

The fans for both sides had become more restless as the game neared the final out. Our fans refused to sit down and they grew louder with every out.

Kory had warmed up in the bullpen, but Julio insisted he was fine in between innings. Even though Coach Wilson wanted to take him out, he knew Julio gave us the best chance to close out the game for a win.

The first batter up was the number four batter in the lineup. After a first pitch strike, the batter grounded weakly to Zach -- out number one.

The next batter worked the count to two balls and two strikes. Jeremy set up outside. Though the ball was thrown in the dirt, the batter swung at it and struck out -- out number two!

In the bleachers, Alexa and Jamie jumped up and down enthusiastically.

The sixth batter in the lineup had not hit the ball all day. Matter of fact, he had been dominated by Julio. Jeremy looked at Coach Wilson, who was near the edge of the dugout. He motioned to Jeremy to keep doing what he was doing.

Jeremy looked at Julio and called for a fastball outside.

Contact was made. The ball drifted into left center field. Julio followed the ball like a radar does a plane.

Julio threw his hands in the air. Jeremy watched the ball as he sauntered towards the mound. Alexa, who was jumping up and down, grabbed onto Jamie's hand and held it tight. As for me, I threw my hands into the air as I began to laugh with excitement.

The ball slowly dropped from the sky into Eric's glove. The game was over and we were the repeat regional champs!

"Congrats to Franklin, the 2013 Regional Champs!" boomed the man in the press box.

Jamie and Alexa jumped up and down enthusiastically.

Jeremy greeted Julio in the middle of the infield and gave him a hug.

"We're going to sectionals!" Julio yelled.

43

Early June

Mike Williams

The bus ride to Cartersville seemed to drag on forever. There were only so many farms, pastures, and corn fields we could look at. Most of us delved into our music devices while others sat and looked out the window.

Zach turned and looked out the back window. He poked Kyle who was in the seat across from him, and motioned with his head out the window. "Looks like we have a following."

Kyle turned. "Holy crap! There must twenty cars back there."

Zach smiled. "I know right!"

As the bus approached the field, we began to frantically put on our solid blue uniforms. Once the bus came to a halt, we quietly walked off the bus one by one. We tried unsuccessfully to hide our smiles when we were greeted with cheers from the Franklin faithful.

Game time finally approached. It was the perfect day for a baseball game.

Like the majority of fans from Franklin, Alexa was

dressed in blue. She found her spot in the lower right corner of the bleachers. Alongside her was Jamie and Stephanie. A few rows back sat Brandy, Kyle's girlfriend. Jamie still struggled to fit in, but to her credit, she tried. I think Alexa did everything she could to make her feel welcome. Stephanie, like Jamie, struggled to fit in since sports wasn't her thing. I was definitely thankful for Alexa. She had a way of welcoming people into her group.

As we ran onto the field, our fans cheered enthusiastically, which, of course, got us amped. Julio must have looked like a giant to many of the Hillsboro players. I know he did to me and I wasn't a small guy.

Julio fell behind the first three batters, but he was able to retire each one.

As he walked into the dugout after the third out, Jeremy greeted him. He put his arm around his big brother. "Relax. You have a kick-butt team on your side. Don't feel you have to do it yourself!"

Julio nodded, though he refused to look at Jeremy.

The bottom half of the inning didn't go any better for our offense. The other team's pitcher was a tall right hander by the name of Jake. If the first inning would be any indication, it would be a low scoring game.

Both pitchers settled in. The game remained scoreless through four innings. Unlike our team, Hillsboro had their chances to score. Two times they had runners on second or third. Thankfully, we were able to get out of the inning without allowing any runs. On the other hand, we were atrocious at the plate.

The first batter in the fifth for Hillsboro was able to get on with a hit up the middle. The next batter up was Derek Sims, one of the best hitters in Southern Illinois. Derek looked to the third base coach who went through a series of signs. Derek stepped into the batter's box.

Jeremy glanced to first base after giving Julio the pitching sign.

Julio stepped into his motion, glanced towards first, and drove towards home with the pitch. The pitch was a ball and the runner stayed. In between pitches, the fans on both sides cheered. If the call was a ball, the Franklin fans would "boo," while the Hillsboro fans would cheer. On the hand, if the pitch was a strike, the Hillsboro fans would "boo," and the Franklin fans would cheer. At third, I found this activity humorous.

Julio gathered his thoughts. He took the next sign from Jeremy and paused. Julio momentarily looked over his shoulder towards first base. As soon as Julio lifted his left leg towards home, the runner took off towards second. The batter watched the pitch whistle by for a strike. Jeremy caught the pitch and sprung to his feet. As if the ball was shot out of a cannon, Jeremy rocketed the ball to second. The runner was caught stealing!

The Franklin fans and dugout players erupted! I stood over at third and pumped my fist. Both coaches pumped their fists in the air as well. Julio looked at Jeremy and smiled. Though Jeremy didn't smile, he acknowledged his brother with a nod.

With one out in the inning, Julio struck the next batter out. The third out was a lazy ground out to Zach at shortstop.

Much to our disappointment, we weren't able to score or even get a runner on base. Girlfriends and parents from both sides struggled to watch the game. It was so close.

Julio cruised through the sixth inning. As he returned to the dugout, he was stopped by Coach Wilson. "Can you finish off the seventh?"

"Of course, Coach. This is my game. We got this." Julio said confidently.

The bottom of the order was up for our team. Hillsboro

decided it was time to take out their starter and put in a reliever.

Zach walked up to me. I was next to Julio on the edge of the dugout. "Boys, we got this guy. The game is yours, Julio. Go at them."

Julio looked at Zach and smiled.

I remained quiet at first. "This guy's nothing. Shit, we better hit him," I eventually muttered.

The first batter, Jeremy, walked up to home plate to hit.

Alexa looked at Jamie. "You nervous?"

Jamie smiled. "Yeah, I don't know how these guys do it."

Alexa laughed. "Yeah, I know. I'd be up there shaking in my heels." She reached for Jamie's hand.

The count deepened to three balls and two strikes. Jamie squeezed Alexa's hand tighter and tighter.

The sixth and final pitch whisked towards home plate. Jeremy swung! Alexa and Jamie, along with everyone around them, jumped to their feet.

The Franklin players ran to the edge of the dugout. Could it be? Would it be? It was! Jeremy just hit a freaken homerun to take the lead!

The Franklin fans erupted as Jeremy crossed home!

Jamie ran to the base of the bleachers. Alexa followed. They both jumped up and down enthusiastically. In her exuberance, Jamie hugged everyone around her.

Inside the dugout, Zach, Julio, and I all looked at each and smiled. I nudged Julio. "Well son of a bitch. Your brother did it."

Julio proudly nodded his head.

Zach tugged on Julio's shirt. "Dude, we need to get out there!"

Jeremy neared home and was greeted by his brother and the rest of the team. We were now up by one.

The game was now in Julio's hands.

As Julio made his way to the mound, he passed Coach Wilson. Coach Wilson smiled and gave Julio a thumbs up.

Julio grinned. "No worries, Coach. I got this."

Julio got the first batter out on strikes. The second batter grounded out to Zach at shortstop. With one out remaining, Julio stepped off the rubber and took a deep breath.

He looked at me. "This is your game. Go get him," I said with a smile.

Not intimidated by the seventh hitter, he struck him out in three pitches.

Game over. We were in the Sectional Finals again!

44

Early June

Mike Williams

The sectional championship game was a hard fought game between us and Williamsburg. We were clearly the better team as we beat them by seven runs. The State Championship was a week away.

Graduation was a blur for many of us who played on the baseball team. It was also a blur for Alexa. Our graduation was the Friday night before our first state playoff game. All through the ceremony, Julio glanced around. It was hard to believe he had lived in Franklin for only two years.

Alexa sat a few rows away from Julio. A tear ran down her cheek. She smiled when she thought about Nicole.

As each student moved across the stage, there was an applause of varying degrees. Some were louder than others. Julio approached the stage as the principal neared his name.

"Julio James" announced our Principal.

To Julio's surprise, many of us cheered. I actually stood up, even though I wasn't supposed to.

Once the ceremony was over many of us wanted to stay up to celebrate, but there was one more task at hand.

The next morning came way too soon. Most of us were restless.

The ride was quiet as the bus passed corn and soybean fields, small towns, and random barns. I never really knew Illinois was so flat! Behind the bus was a long caravan of cars which had become the norm over the past few weeks.

The bus rolled into the Springfield baseball complex. Many of us had never seen this many ball fields in one area.

Prophetstown was our first opponent. From what I was told, if you blinked, you'd miss the town as you drove through. It was that small. Prophetstown did not consist of any superstars, but overall, they had a solid core of good ball players.

The bleachers were packed with fans from both sides. Alexa, Jamie, and Stephanie all rode up together and wore their Franklin blues.

The game went pretty much to script. We wound up winning 3-0. Julio threw five innings and only allowed four hits. Game one was down and we had advanced to the next round. After the game, Julio was greeted by Alexa with a hug.

While Alexa was in his arms, Julio leaned over and whispered, "Just two more games and we are the champs." Alexa smiled and squeezed him tighter.

The ride back to Franklin went much quicker than the ride up. Probably because we won the first game and everyone was in a good mood. By the time we had arrived in Franklin, it was almost midnight. No games were scheduled for the following day thankfully.

The next day, Sunday, Stephanie and I decided to go over to Alexa's house for a few minutes. Of course, Julio was already there when we arrived. I think that was his second home. Julio wandered into Alexa's house for a glass of lemonade.

I followed Julio into the kitchen. "Dude, have you heard anything from any of the pro teams?" I asked curiously.

Caught off guard, Julio spilled his lemonade onto the floor.

"How about a warning next time?" Julio said with a smile.

"Sorry man," I responded amusingly.

Julio leaned up against the counter. "Nah I haven't heard anything from anyone. I know San Francisco was looking at me, but I don't know if they're still interested. I know I signed with Stanford, and though I can get out of it if drafted, there are very few teams I would actually play for now."

I looked at Julio and then back towards the main door. In all honesty, I wanted to talk to Julio, but I didn't want Stephanie to hear our conversation. I wasn't worried about Alexa though. "Yeah. I know St. Louis was looking at me and expressed interest, but, I guess I'm not concerned. Whatever happens, happens. Right?"

Julio nodded. "I am curious. How does Stephanie feel about all of this?"

I took a sip of the lemonade Julio poured for me. "That's why I'm asking. How is Alexa with all of this? Stephanie isn't always the most supportive. Yeah, she doesn't want me to go very far from ole Franklin."

Julio paused. "I don't know what to tell you, man. Just let the dominoes fall where they do. If you get drafted, awesome. Otherwise, go play in college and raise your stock. I mean, if that is what you want to do. It's her doing if she doesn't want to be along for the ride. Don't let her determine your future."

I stood against the side of the door and contemplated what Julio told me.

He looked at me. "Let's win state and then we can worry about everything else. Winning state is something no one can take away from us. Not even a girl."

"Well... thanks for your words, man," I said with a half-hearted smile.

Monday finally came as we made our way back up to Springfield for the semi-final game against Harvard. The town of Harvard was found in the northernmost part of the state just outside of Chicago. In many ways the town was similar to Franklin, just on opposite ends of the state.

Dressed in our all white uniforms, we took the field. The semi-final game had arrived. Kyle was the starting pitcher. He walked out to the mound and was in awe. The mound seemed higher than other mounds he had thrown on. His fastball seemed to have more pop as is crossed home plate.

As the game went deeper, every pitch and out became more important and more intense. Both teams had hard throwers and both lineups were stacked with hitters. The game remained tied up at one through five innings. In the sixth inning, Harvard took the lead to make the score 2 to 1.

In the seventh inning, Harvard did not score any runs even though runners were in scoring position with one out.

In between every pitch, the fans from both sides were loud. Several times Zach and I looked at each other and smiled. Though the game was tight, it was sure fun! The players of Unionville and Shellville stood and watched the game with curious anticipation, since the winner of their game would face the winner of our game.

Alexa couldn't sit down no matter how hard she tried. Jamie was hooked. Even though she was never super competitive, nor a big sports fan, she admittedly looked forward to two more years of this.

We had one more chance to score one run to tie or two to win. Our first three batters were six through eight in the lineup. If anyone was able to get on Shawn, the ninth hitter in the lineup would be due up.

In between innings, Coach Wilson and Coach Jacobs looked at the subs but decided a pinch hitter was out of the question. I guess they came to the conclusion there was no one on the bench better than the hitters due up, which, in all honesty, was true.

Jeremy was the first hitter. Their relief pitcher was tall and threw the ball hard. The first pitch was a ball just outside. Jeremy stepped out of the batter's box and took a deep breath and mumbled to himself. The next pitch was a strike which he fouled off. He fell behind in the count after he whiffed on the third pitch.

Jamie sat on the bleachers and nervously bit her lip and wrung her hands.

The pitcher stepped into his windup. Fooled by the pitch, Jeremy struck out.

One out!

Crap!

The next batter up was Tim Wilson, our left fielder who had replaced Ronald, thankfully. He worked all year to improve and by end of the year he found himself in the starting lineup.

Tim, like Jeremy, wanted to be patient and tried to wait for his pitch. The first pitch was on the outside part of the plate. Strike one. He stepped out of the box to gather his thoughts. He paused to look at his bat. He stepped back into the batter's box. The second pitch came in with a little more movement on it than the first pitch. Again, he swung with no luck and missed. The count was no balls and two strikes. The next two pitches were balls. The count was now two balls and two strikes. Our bench oohed and ahhed.

Harvard fans stomped their feet on the bleachers in between pitches creating a loud rickety noise. I guess they hoped to distract Tim. Whether it worked or not, Harvard was in the lead and just two outs away from victory.

Tim watched the next pitch go by for strike three.

Two outs!

Shit!

The next batter up was our second basemen, Cliff Johnson, another junior on the team who did not play every game.

Cliff took one final practice swing before he made his way to home plate. He looked at Shawn, the next batter up, with a straight face. "Dude, you better get a hit and bring me in. I don't want to be standing out there on base. You hear me?"

Shawn nodded confidently.

Cliff worked the count two balls and no strikes. The third pitch he lined to left field for a hit. Our fans leaped with joy as Cliff rounded first and jogged into second standing up with a two out double.

A double! The tying run was on second!

Shawn walked up to the batter's box. You could tell he was in the middle of an in depth conversation with himself. He was so locked in. I don't think he could even hear our bench or our coaches.

He took a breath.

The first pitch zipped towards home. Shawn's eyes widened as the ball neared home plate.

As soon as it was hit, everyone from our side jumped into a frenzy. Alexa threw her hands into the air and began to yell wildly. Jamie jumped up and laughed nervously.

The left fielder for Harvard took one step back and then stopped to watch the ball. There was no reason for him to go any farther. The ball was gone! We were in the Championship game!

45

Early June

Mike Williams

After our game, we grabbed a bite to eat at one of the local fast food places. Then, we made our way back to the grounds to watch the end of the Unionville versus Shellville game.

Unionville wound up winning, which meant we played them next. The weather couldn't have been better for a late afternoon game. The stands remained full on the Unionville side and our fans stayed for the game as well. Small boys sat next to their dad's. Girlfriends cheered on their boyfriends. Moms squirmed with every pitch. The outfield was scattered with fans as well. Yeah, the environment was pretty cool.

In the third inning, Julio hit a homerun which gave us the lead. Unionville took the lead in the top of the fifth inning. The intensity inside each dugout was palpable.

Kory started the game on the mound and was relieved midway through the game by Julio. In the sixth inning, Coach Wilson took Julio out as the pitcher and put him in right. The batters had hit Julio hard all day and the last thing

Coach wanted to do was keep him in too long. By now, each pitching staff was somewhat depleted. Thankfully, the same could be said for Unionville.

The game remained 6 to 5 Unionville through six innings. The freshmen, Tommy Glover, was called in to pitch while Julio went to right field. Thankfully, the seventh inning went smoothly for us defensively. No one from the Unionville side got on base. Tommy walked into the dugout relieved he had done his part for at least one inning.

Coach Wilson greeted him at the edge of the dugout. "Be ready to go in next inning if we tie this game up."

Tommy nodded his head.

Zach walked up and down the dugout. He did all he could to energize the team. "Let's go! We've gone too far to stop now!"

I walked up to Julio. "Hey man, trust me. We got this game."

Julio looked at me and smiled confidently. "Yeah, we do. This is our time."

Alexa looked at Jamie, who seemed to be un-phased. "How could someone not be excited about this game?"

"I don't know," she replied with a smile as she shrugged her shoulders.

The bottom of seventh started off well. The first two batters got on base. With runners on first and second, Zach stepped up to the plate. This was something he had dreamt of for a very long time.

Our fans stood and cheered for Zach. Down the right field foul line stood Julio's mom and dad. Mrs. James stood nervously in her husband's arms.

After he peered towards third base, Zach took a breath and gathered his thoughts. He stepped up to bat.

The pitcher went into his windup and released the ball. The ball zipped towards home.

PLUNK!

Zach got hit by the ball. Disgusted he got hit, Zach threw down his bat and jogged towards first with his head down. He, of course, was upset he didn't have a chance to get the winning hit.

The bases were loaded for Julio. Can you believe it?! No out and Julio was up.

Our fans paused for a moment and then erupted enthusiastically.

"Bases are loaded and no one's out," yelled Alexa. "Go Julio!"

Julio slowly walked towards home plate. He glanced

towards third base. Coach pumped his fist. "Come on, Julio! This is your chance!"

Julio tapped the handle of his bat with his right hand. He stood with one foot out of the batter's box. After glancing around the field, he took a breath and stepped into the batter's box.

The pitcher stepped into his motion. The first pitch was outside for ball one.

Coach Wilson pumped his fist. "Wait for your pitch! They don't want to walk you!"

Julio stepped out of the box. He took another breath. He stepped into the batter's box for the next pitch.

The next pitch was outside for ball two.

Our bench was in a frenzy in between every pitch. Every player could taste victory, if only Julio could come through. Jeremy stood by himself on the far end of the bench. As for myself, I did my best to focus on my at bat if Julio happened to make an out. I was just too excited!

Alexa looked over to her left and smiled. Her former friend, Janet, was on her feet.

Janet acknowledged Alexa with a smile. Along with everyone around her, Janet began to chant Julio's name as he stepped in for the third pitch of the at bat.

Julio's parents continued to stand by themselves. Mrs. James was so nervous she couldn't watch the game. Instead, Mr. James had to give her a play by play account of the game.

"Okay hun, he's in the box for the third pitch," Mr. James whispered. He continued, "The pitch is delivered."

The fastball was down the middle of the plate.

BANG!

Alexa and all of the other fans from Franklin jumped into the air.

Julio's mom did a 180 degree spin when she heard the bat clank and the fans roar. Mr. James began to laugh uncontrollably as he watched the ball drift in the air towards leftfield.

The Franklin bench erupted like Mount St. Helen. Jeremy threw his arms into the air, while the rest of the players ran around the dugout in search of someone to hug. As for me? Well, I just laid my bat on the ground and watched with admiration as the ball drifted towards left.

Coach Wilson threw his hands into the air in joy as the ball sailed over the fence.

We had just won the State Championship!

Julio ran the bases and smiled.

Alexa ran to the fence and pressed her face up to it. Excited, Jamie followed her. "Julio! Julio!" yelled Alexa.

Julio saw Alexa up next to the fence. He smiled.

Jeremy ran up and gave his brother a hug.

"We did it Jeremy!"

After we all greeted Julio at home we turned towards the backstop and acknowledged our fans. It was cool to hear them chant "We are -- State Champs!"

The Unionville fans, though disappointed, stood and applauded their team as they walked off the field with their heads down.

We finally gathered our equipment after we celebrated in right field. As Julio made his way out of the dugout, he was greeted with a thump in his side from Alexa. She wrapped her arms around him.

Julio noticed Zach and I who were only a few feet away. We both gave him a thumbs up. I mean, we couldn't have done it without him or his brother. Alexa looked to her right and noticed Janet.

"Congratulations," she muttered with a smile as she reached for Julio's hand.

Julio returned the smile. "Thanks, I appreciate it."

The four hour bus ride flew by. Heck, we celebrated the

whole way home. The bus finally rolled into Franklin. We had finally calmed down, more so because we were tired. The bus rolled to a stop.

Coach Wilson stood up. "Guys, I want to say thank you. To the seniors, I hope you come back." He paused. "The seniors have set the standard. Expect us to work even harder next year, because this is a good taste. Lastly, thanks...thanks for making this a fun victory and a fun year. Can you believe we are State Champs?!"

We cheered enthusiastically.

Coach Wilson waited for Julio to get off the bus.

"Julio, come here, son."

Julio approached coach who had his hand out for him. Julio reached out and hugged Coach. Tears streamed down both of their faces.

The next morning, Julio and Jeremy woke up earlier than they had hoped. Julio looked at his brother. "Well, we're awake. Do you want to go for a run?"

Jeremy covered his head with his pillow. "Yeah, I'll go." After a few minutes, the two had their shoes and shorts on.

About midmorning, he and Jeremy made their way over to Alexa's house. She jumped from her swing when she noticed Julio. "Look at you two, the State Champs. I'm surprised you will even talk to me and haven't forgotten about me, Mr. Homerun," she said sarcastically.

Alexa's mom popped her head out and smiled. "Morning, Julio."

"Morning, Mrs. Sherman," Julio said with a grin a mile wide.

Back at Julio's house, the phone rang. "Huh, I wonder who's calling," Mr. James asked out loud since the home phone rarely rang. "It's probably a telemarketer," he huffed.

"Hello?" Mrs. James asked with an air of sarcasm.

On the other end of the phone was a voice she had heard before, but couldn't place. "Hello. May I talk to Julio?"

"Who is this?" She asked.

The man quickly replied. "This is Mike Dripps, lead scout in charge of player operations for the San Francisco Giants. Is your son there? I'm happy to tell you he's been drafted in the first round this morning. He is a part of the organization if he wants."

Nearly spitting up her coffee, Mrs. James stuttered in disbelief. "He's...He's not home right now. He's over at his girlfriend's."

"May I have a number to contact him then?" he asked.

Mrs. James shook with excitement.

After she gave Mr. Dripps Julio's number, she hung up the phone and reached for her cell phone. She quickly texted Julio.

Expect a call.

We were at Alexa's house when Julio's cell phone vibrated. The text from his mom popped up. He shrugged it off. He probably figured he and Jeremy were in trouble for one reason or another.

Each one of us was working on a glass of lemonade enjoying the spring air, when Julio's phone rang.

"Hello?" Julio asked curiously.

"Hey, is this Julio?" the man asked.

"This is."

"Well son, this is Mike Dripps from the Giants organization. Do you remember me? We have talked before and we met face to face this past spring. Do you have a moment? I'm not keeping you from anything, am I?"

"No sir. You're fine," Julio responded.

"Let me cut to the chase. You were our 14th pick in the draft. You're a Giant. That is, unless you'd rather go to Stanford."

"I'm a what?"

"You heard me right, son. You have been drafted by the Giant's organization and I wanted to call and let you know. It's standard practice...We'll get more info to you in the next day via email. We have your parents email as well as yours, so expect some paperwork to read through. Go home and talk about it with your family and your girlfriend."

In disbelief, Julio hung up the phone. He looked at us. "I've been drafted."

Jeremy, Alexa, and I all looked at each other.

Julio stood up and looked at Alexa and Jeremy. He threw his hands in the air. "I've been drafted! I'm a San Francisco Giant!"

Biography

Dave Mayer was born in Illinois and now lives in the Atlanta, Georgia area. He has been a lifelong lover of baseball. For the last twenty years, Dave has been a teacher and coach, both of which have heavily influenced his writing. This is the first book in his series which takes place in the fictional town of Franklin.

Made in the USA
Columbia, SC
23 November 2021